TALES FROM
THE FUR SIDE

Purrfectly Adorable Cat Stories

Peter Benn

Argosy Media

Paperback ISBN: 978-0-9873337-5-9

eBook ISBN: 978-0-9873337-2-8

Editor: Anthea Wynn

Published by Argosy Media

Postal: PO Box 7615, MELBOURNE, Victoria 3004 Australia

Email: info@peterbenn.com

For those of us who know that our cats

are a whole lot smarter, observant

and spiritually aware than we

doting humans believe possible.

A Welcome Meow

TALES FROM THE FUR SIDE is a wide-ranging collection of short stories as told by a series of my fellow raconteur cats - cats that are wise through experience, thoughtful through reflection, spiritual through ancestry and amusing through their association with a variety of humans.

As humans you see the world through human experiences.... and always from a height of around six feet from the ground. Your frantic lives, your penchant for hurrying, your lack of time for reflection, your self-centered focus, your race for material possessions....

That, unfortunately, is your world, but that is not the world of the cat.

Mine is a world of sleeping, eating, playing, observing, and then sleeping some more. We do not work, nor hurry - there is calm and curiosity. We are independent, choose our own home environment, expect to be looked after and enjoy our nine lives to the full.

Nor do we make war. Spread lies. Covet another's possessions. Or have need for money.

Like the inner you, we adore happiness and contentment. But we, too, grieve for lost family, for the injured and the lonely. We are very forgiving, and ask for little more than shelter, two meals a day and a tolerance to our lifestyle.

Whilst you have been frantically 'living' your life we have been observing your world and we believe that now is the time for us to share with you some of the Ancient Wisdoms to which we have been privileged.

So come with an open heart and a tolerant soul, and see your world afresh.

And perhaps, as humans, you might also then view each other with a little more tolerance, humanity and understanding. That is our hope.

With love and blessings.

Your Feline Friends

 # The Cat's Revenge

It is part of a cat's inalienable right to live, love and play wherever it chooses and with whomsoever it chooses to share. We have inherited a love for freedom that is as important as the heritage the pioneers carved in the human world.

Take myself, for example. I choose to live most of my life with my mistress in a lovely big house in a charming leafy suburban neighborhood. I am pleased to say that she treats me with all the luxury that she can afford, and I of course, respond in grateful appreciation.

But, as a cat with a pioneering spirit, I also have the urge to move around my neighborhood, calling on friends (both human and feline) tasting the bountiful foods and milks that are offered to me and generally keeping an eye open for opportunities for fun and adventure and doubtless, a little mischief making.

And so it was on this particular day that I sauntered off along the rear fence, across the oak and into the first of the neighborhood yards. A favorite pre-occupation with me is to tease as many canines as possible. This, of course, is very easy to do, particularly as so many of them are without a vestige of a brain. They act like lemmings going over a cliff!

Roger, the Bulldog at Number 25 is just such a case in point. Roger couldn't even waddle to the edge of the cliff to save himself, let alone have the ability to see the cliff edge through those puffed up bags of eyes. And his manners! Oh, my dear! Dripping saliva wherever he goes. Hardly the image required to be rescued from eternal bachelorhood. Being so dim witted, a quick walk along his fence or a hiss from a lower branch of the magnolia tree is all that is required to have him barking for hours.

By the time I had strutted my stuff at Number 39 and over-excited the terrier of old Mr. Samuels, it seemed that the whole neighborhood was a cacophony of irrational doggie vocal indulgence.

From my perch high up in the oak tree I had a commanding view of the local back yards. Many of the doggie owners were outside trying to see what had caused all the commotion, and in each case, trying to pacify their canine companion. But they saw nothing. As you know, we felines are far too adept at covering our tracks, and have the ability to move wherever we want to, silently and swiftly.

But the most irate of these doggie owners was old Mr. Samuels. He paced that back yard of his shouting revenge to whoever would listen. No one was in sight, and he certainly couldn't see me, but with his walking stick waving in the air and the tone of his voice decidedly at the 'angry' end of the barometer, he was declaring war. No cat was ever going to upset his dog again. And with that declaration, both he and the yapping terrier disappeared inside the house.

Such threats had been heard before from others, and nothing had transpired. But little did I suspect what he had in store for me.

Old Samuels was willing to try anything to keep cats from his yard, so it was with a victorious glee that he spread the evil smelling little green pellets throughout his entire garden.

"Bye, bye, pussies" he sang out loud. "Puss off to someone else's garden. Be seeing you. Ha. Ha. Ha."

It took him most of the afternoon, but by early evening he had accomplished his mission. Looking down from the oak you couldn't see the little pellets, but my, oh my, the stench that rose from that garden was decidedly foul! Certainly this was no place for cats like myself.

That night from my comfortable bed I could hear the news of the day traveling around the feline neighborhood.

"Have you smelt the garden at Number 39?" a voice meowed.

"Yes, worse than my masters old jogging shoes," jokingly replied another.

"So what are we going to do about it?" was the big question every moggy was asking. "Old Samuels needs to be taught a lesson, but how?"

I hadn't easily taken to sleep that night, so out through my cat-door and into the night I went. On the breeze, even at my house, there was just a waft of that evil smell. It grew more intense as I slinked towards Number 39. It seemed that just about all of the feline locals who could sneak away from their home had gathered near the offending house.

Discussion was heated but unanimous, that Samuels had to be shown the evil of his ways. Whilst every cat would try to think up a plan, it was agreed that we would at least begin our campaign with a neighborhood sing-along throughout the night.

There were about seventeen cats there that night, so we spaced ourselves evenly around the two sides and the rear of the property, with some up trees and others sitting on the fences.

If I do say so myself, it was one of the most successful sit-ins we local cats have ever organized. The caterwauling, meowing, and other radical noises emanating from far and near from midnight to nearly dawn had all the desired effects. Not only did we have a good time, we succeeded in having three objects hurled at us from different households and received verbal abuse too obnoxious to mention. We irritated the entire canine neighborhood into constant uproar and Old Samuels' light was frequently on and off throughout the night.

Just before daylight, with one joint caterwaul to the moon

for good luck, we ended the sit-in going back to our own homes to try and get the bad odor out of our throats and fur, and to make plans for our revenge.

I awoke to the sound of my mistress looking very bleary-eyed talking to a neighbor on the telephone.

"It was nearly as bad down here," she said. "Hardly got a wink of sleep all night."

I admit that it is a little hard to look wide-eyed and bushy tailed at that time of the morning, especially after a hard night out with the neighbors, but we felines are actors after all. I felt pleased when I heard her say that I had obviously *not* been part of such goings on as I was wide-awake and ready to start my day. You humans are so easily fooled! I could sleep the whole day whilst she was at work. As indeed I did!

Whilst I drifted in and out of sleep that afternoon, a series of plans came and went in my mind. I needed a plan that would cause maximum embarrassment with minimum harm.

By late afternoon the germ of a master plan had been sown. It was time to talk to the other cats about it. My mistress wasn't due home until late, so this was the ideal time to get the others over for a meeting.

The whole eight of them were very impressed with my automatic self-feeding container that allows tasty nibble bits to tumble into the bowl with a seemingly never-ending supply. No wonder when my mistress is away, my friends like to come through the cat door and pay me a visit. There are rules, of course. Like, no clawing the newly upholstered lounge suite, or muddy paw marks on the polished floorboards, but other than that, every cat is made to feel at home. So long as there was no evidence of a visitation, our afternoon soirees could continue unabated.

At this meeting, one cat was on top of the television set, another on the second level of the bookcase. Others were spread comfortably on the settee and armchairs, another beside the orchid. And of course, myself, as convener, sat centre stage on the Chippendale (we cats do appreciate the finer things of life. On behalf of all my brethren, "thank you" dear reader for these little luxuries).

"Huhumm," I gently coughed. "Let's begin."

"Has anyone come up with a plan?" I asked, knowing full well that democracy must not only be seen to be done, whilst secretly aware that no one could possibly have thought up such a dastardly revenge as I had! And, except for the anticipated ideas of a mass excreta sit-in, another night or two of mass caterwauling and jumping on Samuels as he walked under his tree to collect his morning newspaper, there were no workable suggestions.

"OK. Here's what we'll do," I stated categorically. "Samuels has to be made to be embarrassed in front of his neighbors. He has to be shown to be the cat hater that he is so that all our owners will feel reviled by his actions and make him clean up his evil smelling yard."

"But how?" was the question that emanated from the top of the television set.

"Well, we are all actors. What we have to do is show our masters and mistresses that we are being made ill from Samuel's little green nasties.

"Now this is how it will be orchestrated," I stated.

My aim was to get as many cats involved as possible, each attracting a human who would carry our cause a little further.

Pusscat was the first cat on the schedule. She was to stagger out of Samuels' front gate, feign chronic pain and attract a gullible human who just happened to be passing by.

This she did extraordinarily adeptly. The limp back leg dragging on the path, the agonized meow, and adding her own engaging professional touch - the tongue hanging out slightly to one side of the mouth.

The postman on his bicycle and the passing pedestrian didn't stand a chance!

As the Postman bent down and lifted Pusscat gently into his half empty postbag, he told the pedestrian that he was going straight to the vet. At that moment I realized for sure that our bold plan would succeed.

As soon as this newly commandeered two-wheel animal

ambulance was out of sight, it was the turn of Mr. Beau.

Now, his acting ability wasn't up to the same standard as that of Pusscat but even so, he could cough and dry reach with the best of them. Even the thought of a 'cleansing' dose of castor oil at the vets didn't deter his enthusiasm. Miss Smythe, from Number 18, observed this coughing phenomena, and right on cue, was soon running up Samuels' path to aid the victim.

"My dear, what has he done to you, you poor thing?" she enquired of no one in particular.

Mr. Beau's innate sense of the theatric was further enhanced by a number of the green pellets he had thoughtfully, and at great cost to his sense of smell, pushed to the pathway near where he was performing. Miss Smythe was quick to observe 'the facts', and was soon comforting Mr. Beau in one arm whilst knocking on Samuels' door with great gusto. No one answered of course, because Thursday was Samuels and his dog's day out.

"I must take you to the vet immediately," said Miss Smythe, and was quickly bundling a bemused, but still coughing Mr. Beau into her car.

"Two out of two" I chuckled to myself from my hiding place high up in the tree that spread out from Samuel's garden and over the pedestrian path. "Now for the triple."

I had to wait until just after noon for our pièce de résistance to be enacted, naturally with me as the star performer.

Other cats were also rostered as 'extras' into this scenario in various parts of the front garden where they would play dead, cry in agony or generally look sick.

Each afternoon, television news reporter Janice Featherstone would call to see her mother who lived two doors along from Samuels' house. She would park the Network's news van under my tree, and walk the few steps to her mother's home.

Humans are creatures of habit, and fortunately for us, that day was no exception. Right on time, Ms Featherstone stepped out of her vehicle and began her short walk. I waited for the right moment.... and dropped.

Her primal scream pierced the stillness of the neighborhood, interrupting many a tranquil luncheon.

I had dropped like a dead weight onto her body and fallen like a stone onto the grass at her feet. It could be said that I did overdo the death scene just slightly, but I still maintain to this day that the point had to be made in the most dramatic way possible!

I, too, used the gasping for air, deep pool eyes and drooping tongue techniques, all to brilliant effect. As neighbors came running from all directions, I was the centre of attention. And how fortunate that at that very moment the vet, the postman and Miss Smythe all arrived to further share in the unfolding story. The other principal feline actors all played their parts beautifully, each, as they were discovered, adding more detail to the emerging dastardly scenario of old Mr. Samuels.

Rarely have I witnessed such a genuine outpouring of sympathies for the feline world as I saw that day.

With such an emotional sidewalk gathering it was only natural that in time the police would arrive.

A knock on the door confirmed that Samuels wasn't at home, so the two police officers began their investigation of the garden without him. The hot noonday sun added a new dimension to our cause. Soon the smell of those pellets began wafting like acrid smoke amongst the perfumes of the many flowers. Those that had been pushed on to the pathway during our little drama were now like gooey green mounds of melting chlorophyll.

And the more the police and the vet investigated, the more horrified they became.

"There are enough pellets in this yard not only to scare off every cat in the suburb, but they contain enough poison to kill a whole city of cats," exclaimed the vet. A superbly timed cough and a wheeze from the two nearby cats reinforced the observation.

"Then every one of the pellets will have to be picked up and removed from the property," declared the newly arrived Health Inspector. "But by who?" the police asked.

Just then it was the 'misfortune' of Samuels and that canine shadow of his, to arrive home.

The television news crew got to him first, asking him about his attitude towards cats, would he like to have poison pellets scattered throughout the interior of his home and was he planning to come back to earth in his next life as a cat? The neighbors, the postman, the vet, the police and a bevy of local cats continued the volley of abuse towards the man. The dog had quietly disappeared to the back of the garden without so much as a whimper, again proving that they are all bluff with no stomach for a good fight.

Finally, this gaggle of human enthusiasm railroaded Samuels into agreeing to begin that very afternoon to pick up and dispose of every one of the dastardly pellets. And furthermore, to promise to never, ever, again use any substance that would harm or intimidate their cats.

As I sit here up his tree, I can see Samuels, gloves on hands, down on all fours, working his way along the garden beds at the side of the house. Standing near him as supervisor and self-appointed warden is dear, dear Miss Smythe. Not a pellet has escaped her attention - as she is quick to point out to her victim.

And through the window of a neighbor's house I can see the beginning of the early evening television news.

"Local cats saved from bizarre deaths by newsroom staff," it begins.

And tomorrow's newspapers, what will they make of the story....

"NOT IN MY GARDEN!" vows cat killer,

"MYSTERY ILLNESS SWEEPS SUBURB - Cat Killer Unmasked" or

"KILLER STALKS NEIGHBORHOOD - The Facts."

But now for a little doze, for I know that tonight is going to be a long one. When the moon is high, the revelry will begin. Tonight we will sing the victory of the common cat. Tonight we will feast and be merry. Tonight we will be cats in celebration.

Let no human underestimate us.

Let no one sleep!

 # Trapped!

For centuries we felines have lived with your ancestors in houses at or near ground level. But today, your architects and engineers and investors seem to agree that going skyward is the best way to build. Reach for the heavens. Build tall monuments of glass and steel. Let the ego run riot in a dizzying race to be the highest.

Now, that is not to say that we cats don't like the world of high-rise apartment living - quite the contrary. But it can be fraught with dangers - dangers that you humans overlook.

Take for example, the Christmas before last. My mistress was flying off to a warmer climate, to a country where cats were not welcome unless they stayed caged, incarcerated in a concrete and wire pen for weeks on end. She was going on a walking holiday and would be incommunicado for much of the time.

Wisely, (I thought at the time), my mistress made arrangements for me to stay in an apartment in the heart of the city belonging to a business friend of hers.

On the appointed day my carry-cage was duly made ready. The soft padded quilt was placed on the floor of it, and to one side, a number of my favorite playthings - a mouse with a bell in its stomach, a ball of orange wool and a little white table-tennis ball. My favorite china bowls were also carefully packed into my traveling bag, along with the usual array of medicines, brushes, cans of 'approved' foods, story books and music discs. My mistress has learned very well how to cater for my many whims and capricious demands.

And it gave me inward pleasure to hear her extolling to her friend the virtues of my breed and the consequent joys of looking after me. Then she went through my daily routine several times just to be sure that I was going to be left in good hands. With a big hug and a kiss, my mistress said goodbye to me, and placed me gently into the carry-cage. Jennifer (my new host) delicately lifted up my cage and travel pack, and we were gone.

Even though the outside air was close to freezing and the wind could be heard whistling around the outside of the car, inside it was warm and cozy. Jennifer liked classical music and this played on the car radio. She talked to me about Christmas, and present buying, and the weather, and her plans for enjoying the next few days away from work. As she had been instructed, my cage was placed on cushions in the front seat, high enough for me to enjoy the view as we traveled along. All in all it was a very pleasant drive, and Jennifer was obviously already very adept at ensuring that my every whim was going to be catered for. "Yes," I thought to myself, "this is going to be a very pleasant vacation."

I shouldn't have looked up! When she said 58th floor, I simply shouldn't have looked up!

Through the gloom of the late afternoon light I could see this enormous tower of concrete and steel reaching for the sky.

"Count them," she said. "58 floors up, and we are still not even near the top of the building." And foolishly I did begin to count. But by level 18, or thereabouts, my mind had begun to blur, my heart was pounding and this cat wasn't so sure about his sense of security any more. It was only Jennifer's reassuring stroking of my head that kept me in a reasonable frame of mind.

"We'll drive into the car-park, and then go straight up in the elevator to the apartment" she said.

Will I ever forget my first elevator ride? Not if I live through ten lives!

What ghastly thrill do you humans get from having your stomach drop to some point close to your ankles? And then there's that feeling that I suspect is akin to freefall parachuting where one's whole chest cavity freezes in motionless expectation of arrival? This cat, at least, very nearly gave up one of its lives on that first skyward journey!

I kept trying to make it up to her for days afterwards, but Jennifer shouldn't have put her hand near me between the fourth and the sixth floors. When cats are in a state of crisis we revert to natural forms of defense, and claws help protect us. The doctor said there would be no permanent scarring so I don't understand why she was so miffed about the whole incident. The security guard who answered her screams had also very kindly organized the doctor to visit whilst the neighbors enthusiastically cleaned up the blood on the carpet outside our door.

After three days, the emotional air remained as cold and frosty inside the apartment as the winter weather was outside. I had free reign of the apartment, but we both kept a considerable distance from each other.

It was Christmas Eve, and Jennifer was spending the day on her computer writing email messages to her many friends and business associates across the world. Occasionally she would go into the internet and seek out information that interested her about music or fashion. Christmas music played softly on the radio. The Christmas tree was in the far corner of the room, its lights twinkling, a scattering of neatly wrapped presents beneath its foliage.

I was perched high up on a ledge above the central heating from where I had a commanding view of both inside and outside the apartment. Outside was cold and wintry, the windblown snowflakes scudding around the buildings. From up here on the 58th level I could look out on what seemed like forever. I was in the highest building in the city, and from my perch the antlike humans far below were hurrying in all directions to finish their Christmas shopping. Outside was definitely no place for a feline. This cat was staying put!

Just as I was dozing after my early afternoon nibbles, the telephone rang. The conversation was a brief one, but with pointed questions seeking urgent answers. Jennifer was visibly upset as she hurriedly collected her overcoat from the closet, threw a few items of clothing into an overnight bag, swung her handbag over her shoulder, checked for her keys and left the apartment with a dramatic closing of the door.

That afternoon I dozed and dreamed of warm spring days, of luxuriating under tropical foliage on some far distant shore, of an endless supply of full-cream milk, of listening to my mistress read to me my favorite cat-tales, of chasing slow, dim-witted mice across a kitchen floor. Dreams, dreams, dreams. How divine they make the senses!

By the time I awoke it was dark and cold outside, and snowing heavily. The apartment was still and quiet except for the background music from the radio. The lamps were on, as was the computer. Jennifer had not returned, and therefore there was no food or milk waiting for me. Strange that she should leave so quickly...and without so much as a beg your pardon. I knew that the atmosphere wasn't very cordial, but to leave me unattended, in unfamiliar surroundings, and without food, was unforgivable. My mistress would hear of this, I promised myself.

The evening news services on the radio came and went. The Christmas music continued. The snow flurries ebbed and flowed on the winds outside the window. But thanks to the central heating, the apartment stayed warm and cozy.

As I peered out into the gloom, thoughts of how other cats would be celebrating the festive season came into my mind. Aunt Harriet would no doubt be enjoying the good life at her sunshine retirement village. Uncle Max would be strolling the bright lights of the city theatres, and renegade cousin Phil traipsing the lanes and byways of the underworld. And to add insult to injury, my mistress would be sunning herself on that warm, tropical island.

And what of the many orphan cats in the various animal shelters across the nation? No doubt, they would be soon be joined by many others as the unwanted and unloved feline Christmas presents were lodged, dumped or left at the shelter doors.

That night, that Christmas Eve, high above the commerce of the city, alone in the luxury of warmth and quality possessions, there was an ache in my heart - an ache that was caused by anger or loneliness or fear (I know not which). I thought of the great need within us all, human or feline, to be part of the continuum of life, a fellow traveler on the journey, and not a discarded onlooker watching the passing parade.

I was alone, deserted for whatever reason, with no human or animal companionship, no food, unknown to another soul as being alone and having no way to attract attention. I seemed to have the best view in the world, but all that amounted to naught.

It was a long, lonely Christmas Eve, just the radio and the

computer screen for company. I was warm from the central heating, and continued to doze throughout the night interrupted only by a necessary visit or two to the cat box in the bathroom.

By morning, there was still no Jennifer or other human company to feed me. There were noises of excited children in the outside hallway, but my fretful "Meows" failed to carry through the apartment walls. Outside I could just hear the sounds of the church bells calling the faithful to worship. The radio news talked of the worst snowstorm for generations. The city was paralyzed. The airport closed.

I was alone, abandoned, lost!

Christmas Day and night passed without incident. No visitors, just the occasional message left on the telephone answering machine. The radio continued to tell of the chaos in the outside world. And my tummy began to tell me in no uncertain terms that it was time for tea.

By the end of day two it was becoming obvious that something had to be done to either find food, or to draw attention to one's plight.

The kitchen was the obvious beginning. Jennifer was an immaculate housekeeper. Everything had its place, and as a quick glance indicated, everything was in that place - safe and secure inside the cupboards. Even the refuse bin was orderly, having been emptied only a short time before her departure. No luck there!

Next stop, the Christmas tree, and all those parcels underneath. Surely one of them would have some kind of food. Frankly, I wouldn't have said so before this incident, but small children and hungry cats do have a lot in common when it comes to a destructive approach to opening presents. Claws and teeth are two implements that have been tried and tested – and if I do say so myself, three rampaging pre-school children couldn't have done a better demolition job on the presents than this lone hungry cat.

Sadly, such an effort produced little in the way of tangible results. A bag of salted peanuts, three different boxes of chocolates (poisonous to we felines), some soft sugary jello type jubes and a packet of mixed dried glace fruit - hardly the gourmet delights that this puss had in mind! Still, spilt across the carpet, and mingled with the myriad of pieces of paper, it did allow the odd lick or two to take place. Mind you, it was also fortunate that the bathroom faucet was producing a drip or two, particularly after the meal of salted peanuts and jubes.

After another snooze or two, it seemed timely to bring out the big guns in the way of ideas. As I sat there on the edge of the couch licking the sugar off my paws, it occurred to me that somehow I needed to communicate with the outside world – urgently. There was no way I could physically escape from the apartment, so I needed to get someone to come to me.

I could start a fire - but what if no one came. Trapped on the 58th floor. Was choking to death from smoke inhalation worse than dying from hunger? "YES," I thought, quickly giving up that idea.

Start a flood - water seeping under a doorway and down the stairs would surely bring attention. But how many weeks would it take to fill the bath to overflowing from the volume of drips currently being leaked? No go on that idea.

Use the telephone - well I've seen the television series and I know that the emergency services are very efficient, but would a frantic "Meow" or two down a telephone line be enough to locate me, and to bring them running? A brilliant idea, I thought, but the language barrier stalled that idea in its tracks.

What else? What e-l-s-e?

Slowly I looked around the room. And then my eyes fell upon the key to my salvation. The computer was still winking away at me. Was it still connected to the internet or to her email?

Now, we cats are very much more knowledgeable than we let you humans think, and no doubt I will receive a strong reprimand from the Furfathers for telling you this closely guarded secret. But we quietly watch you humans as you go about your business, and it will be a big surprise to most of you that your saying about quietness catching the mice is in fact, a truism. Quietly watching you gives us the knowledge we need to stay informed and one step ahead of you. We absorb and understand the language of our family provider and can generally read a lot of what you write. We don't have a great need to divulge this knowledge because you are so busy looking after our every whim that if you knew of our superior intellect, you would try to capitalize on it and ruin what is a very comfortable master and servant relationship.

So, with a skip and a jump I was over to the computer desk. The screensaver was producing endless shoals of colorful fish (very pleasant viewing on long, wet afternoons) but with a touch of the mouse (can you explain why it isn't called a rat, a piggy or a turtle?) the screen burst into life. Yes! Yes! We have email. Now, where were her email addresses? Think! Think! (If only my tummy could stop that incessant rumbling.)

In her diary? No, no.

In the printed address book on the shelf? No, that was clipped shut.

Oh dear!

Can you reach "911" Emergency on email I wondered?

Tap, tap, tap with my paw on the "0". No response.

But wait, a new window appeared on the screen....

"THIS NUMBER IS NOT RESPONDING.

DO YOU WANT THE ADDRESS BOOK?

PRESS Y or N

As you can imagine it is not easy for a cat with a wide flat paw to press the exact key he requires without a great deal of three footed juggling. However, a long, downward inclined claw does assist in the process and, with practice, can be most precise. I wasn't going anywhere that day, so after a few concentrated minutes on the keyboard and you would have thought me an expert.

With a claw on the Y key, a gentle press, and before you could shout "furballs", up came all the email addresses. Voilà!

So there I was, alone in this 58th level apartment, sitting on a desk intently staring at a list of names and numbers on a computer screen trying to decide who I wanted to be rescued by. Honestly, if I hadn't been there at the time you probably wouldn't believe that these events took place.

A, B, C, D, E ...

Ah! "FRONT DESK" email address complete with telephone number.

"Use highlight key to put this address in to your email" beamed the computer.

"Hey, this is so simple even a cat can operate it," I murmured to myself. Perhaps the manufacturers could bring out a whole new range of cat-friendly computers named after fish, rather than fruit. I can just imagine the cats of the world using a "SARDINE" or a "SALMON".

With a flick of the highlight key, I had the blank email page up on screen complete with the FRONT DESK address on it as well as my (I mean, Jennifer's) address attached to the message.

And now to write the message... ummmm!

"Help! Being held hostage. Need food – especially lobster. URGENT! Love, Jennifer"

or would this be more appropriate

"Hi Sugarplum,

Am all alone. Champagne getting warm. Send two security men IMMEDIATELY! Suite 58A"

"Wicked! Wicked! Wicked!" I chuckled to myself. Oh, such power at one's command.

Finally, of course, commonsense prevailed. I had to write a message that was going to bring instant action and appropriate food. So I thought long and hard and finally came up with...

HELP! HELP!

Have been kidnapped and left to die in Suite 58A.

Send milk and smoked salmon before it is too late. Hurry.....

Now, how was I to know that the "A" key would send the message to *everyone* in Jennifer's email address book, and not just to that nice security man downstairs? So much concern, and so much excitement!

Of course, after all the kafuffle and confusion died down I found myself being treated like royalty, just as it should have been all along. Everyone wanted to look after me. The media wanted to know how it was that I was able to send the message. Was I the contemporary equivalent of a famous talking horse from television's early years and would I soon have my own similar television series? And Jennifer.... well, it took two additional days and her photograph on national breakfast television before she could be located.

When calm was restored, and I had a spare moment to myself, I felt compelled to write and send one more devilish message, this time to my mistress who was still traveling and totally unaware of what had transpired.....

> Hello My Dear,
>
> I don't want you to worry, but I inadvertently forgot about your cat, and left him locked up in my apartment without food or milk for four days. Have just explained it all on national television. He's eating again, and should be back to his normal weight in a couple of weeks. I repeat, DON'T WORRY! Have a good vacation.
>
> Love and apologies, Jennifer

With a wink and a blink, the message was sent.

This cat was going to live like royalty for a very long time to come!

The Bijou Cinema Cat

Being a cinema cat is not as easy as you might think.

Great Uncle Gustavus had been a cinema cat as long as any of the family could remember. His tales of the movies, and the patrons who attended them, were legendary at family gatherings. After dinner, surrounded by all the kittens, he would extol tall tales and sometimes true, that had each of his listeners enthralled to the last frame. His stories were told very much like a movie unfolding before you, and as the listener, you added your own magic ingredient of imagination. He supplied the framework of the story, complete with meows and purrs running the entire gamut of emotion. Gable or Cruise, Dietrich or Streep, he could voice them all, and what's more, could act out all the famous scenes. Many, many hours had been spent watching the silver screen, and even more watching midnight television repeats. His send-up performance of the exploits of several famous screen dogs invariably dissolved both kitten and cat into uncontrolled fits of hysteria.

It was therefore with some awe that I found myself walking up the marble steps of the picture palace to meet him. Not the cement-box, suburban, multi-cinema complex for him. Oh, no siree! This was your genuine, Depression built, brick and plaster palace of dreams, complete with Upper Circle, Balcony, Stalls, statues, red velvet curtains, palm fronds, theatre organ, chandeliers and seemingly acres of marble.

As you stepped from the banality of the outside streetscape, up the three steps and in through the row of spotlessly clean glass doors, you knew that you were leaving behind the ordinary and the everyday. Here was your own dream-machine, a place where you could be transported to anywhere on earth or beyond, in any time period, without danger or fear, all for the cost of a few dollars, or at no cost whatsoever if you were the cinema cat.

The marble was cold under paw, but a welcome relief from the hot sidewalk I'd encountered coming to the cinema. I took a glance skyward, and there above me, hanging high overhead was the most marvelous chandelier, aglow with lights, radiating a welcoming ambience to those entering the building. Ahead of me was the ticket box, complete with coming attraction posters either side, a glass front with a big round service hole in it and the most wonderful grandmotherly lady sitting waiting to serve.

"You must be the replacement Cinema Cat," she said, as she smiled sweetly down at me. "I'll get Gus for you."

"Replacement? Replacement? I've only come for afternoon tea," I stammered, but she was gone, and had obviously not heard a word I'd purred.

Whilst I waited for Great Uncle Gustavus I looked around me, totally bewitched by the atmosphere of the cinema. There on the wall was a photograph of the two young men who had restored the theatre, and now ran two movies a night, with a different program every day of the week. It was obvious that they loved their creation and shared this love and pride and passion with all of their patrons. The golden stair-rail glowed in the light as if saying to the patrons "leave your troubles at the foot of the stairs, follow me, and I will take you to the other side of your imagination."

In our cities we have just about every type of shopping and entertainment experience imaginable, yet it seems to me that none has yet equaled, or even come near, the spell that a good cinema can cast over its patrons. Where else do you eagerly pay money to buy something you can't hold or carry home, something to which your total knowledge is based on the promise of a poster or a friend's recommendation, where you have to sit in the dark to enjoy it, which you can only experience when someone else says it's the right time and which you have to share it with a group of total strangers?

In a very short time Great Uncle arrived, invited me for a bowl of milk and told me of his dilemma. He needed a holiday and was wondering if I could take his place just for a couple of weeks. Needless to say, with a tummy full of milk (the owners served an excellent full cream variety) combined with the spell of the cinema, no self-respecting cat could refuse.

"When could you start?" he enquired.

And so the following Thursday I officially became the "BCC", the "Bijou Cinema Cat".

The list of jobs and expectations were much larger than I had anticipated:

Bijou Cinema Cat

DUTY STATEMENT

Page 1.

- Sit attentively at the Box Office during the evening selling period

- Must be well groomed, awake, and remain beyond the reach of patrons wishing to pat

- An occasional wink and/or purr is encouraged

- Keep the cinema free of rodents at all times

- Bring to the attention of management any patron or staff misdemeanors

- Be available for a public relations stroll through the foyers during interval (Children's matinee performances excluded) always remembering,

"A Bijou Cat is a Happy Cat!"

Page 2.

- Confine consumption of all food and milk to non-public areas

- Periods of each day to be spent in the cinema window display (awake or asleep is at your discretion)

- At all times to maintain the dignity, hospitality and tradition of the Cinema Cat Guild

Remember our motto:

"A friendly paw is a box office draw"

By Order, The Management

I surmised that to do my job as efficiently as possible I had better familiarize myself a little more with the layout of the old cinema and to meet my fellow human (there being no other feline) members of staff.

Downstairs on the ground level there were the Stalls, the cheapest seats. They were comfortable, covered in a washable velvet and aligned along great arcs across the floor, thus giving all patrons an uninterrupted view as they looked upward to the screen.

Upstairs seating was the Circle, the place where you could see and be seen. You entered via the plush Grand Circle foyer area and then walked up a series of steps. As you reached the top of the steps you had the feeling of going to heaven, it was all so beautiful. You could then move either downwards towards the screen or turn, and climb higher towards the projection portholes. Every seat had thick, comfortable upholstery using luxurious red velvet that gave an effect that this was *your* special chair, your vehicle to transport you to wonders yet unknown.

Around the walls were plaster figures modeled on those found in ancient Grecian temples, periodically interspersed with huge red velvet drapes. Each statue was accentuated by subtle lighting so that it would blend with the equally subtly lit grand red velvet curtain hiding the screen. High above was the ceiling, molded and decorated by some long forgotten descendants of Michelangelo or Raphael. There were cornices, niches, tableaux, roses, borders - a dazzling display of an art form recent enough to be out of fashion, but not old enough to be historic. As the lighting changed through the evening, so it etched out ever-changing patterns and shapes that let the eye wander skyward and be absorbed, like watching clouds on a summer's afternoon.

Also from the Grand Circle foyer there were other doors that were so well disguised into the elaborate wall moldings that patrons had no idea they existed. As well as storerooms and access to various areas behind the walls, one door led to the projection room. And it was there that I met Jake.

Jake was not the original projectionist. That honor belonged to his father, but even as a boy, Jake spent most of his spare time helping to rewind the films, displaying the coming attraction posters, threading the projectors and all the while keeping his nose in various books about films, or the actors and actresses that appeared in them.

When he sat me down with a saucer of milk whilst he drank his coffee, I discovered that Jake was a walking authority on the history of the movies. Talk! Goodness me, he could talk. But what wonderful tales he told. Of sitting alone in the cinema watching Garbo talk for the first time. Of seeing seven little dwarves dance across a colored screen. Of sitting in a crowded Roman amphitheatre cheering a dozen charioteers. Of dancing in the rain, and traveling to galaxies far, far away, of taking 80 days to see the world, and having breakfast at a New York jewelry store. All this and more, all seen on the giant cinema screen, with crystal clarity and full stereo sound.

"It sure isn't television," I mused to myself.

But I had a job to do, so I gave Jake a polite "Meow", licked my lips in appreciation of his hospitality and wandered off knowing full well that I was going to spend many happy hours in his company.

In the halcyon days of the cinema, much of the first half of the program was live entertainment. This could include a cinema organ recital; variety acts like comedians, jugglers, novelty animal acts and acrobats, an orchestra and of course, high stepping dancers. A newsreel, cartoons, travelogues and trailers for coming attractions would follow, with the feature film screening after intermission.

To accommodate these live performers, there were a myriad of under-stage hallways and dressing rooms, as well as corridors created between the internal cinema structure and the outside brick walls. This gave access to all parts of the cinema without staff and performers being seen by the patrons. The corridors had fallen into disrepair through neglect, as they were now redundant to the functioning of the cinema. But to me they were exciting time-tunnels just waiting to be explored.

Over the first couple of days I spent a lot of time wandering these secret passages, chasing the occasional rat, disentangling myself from the ever-present cobwebs, peering stage-struck at the yellowing and curling photos of bygone performers staring down at me from the forlorn make-up mirrors. Here was a musty, cobweb-covered moment in time, frozen with pixie dust, awaiting a prince to kiss it back to life. I deduced that the fairy-tale one hundred years was going to be a long wait.

One of my favorite sleeping spots was high up in the arch of the proscenium where a little plaster had long ago fallen to the floral carpet in the stalls. From here I could look down into the cinema and spend endless hours watching the faces of the patrons. A good movie should totally involve you in its story so that you become oblivious to others around you. One such movie screening that week was an old favorite I'd seen on television (dare I admit it), with lots of creepy moments, dramatic edits, relentlessly moving towards a rattling, high tension climax in a British concert hall. Knowing where most of the tension-releasing moments were placed gave me great pleasure as I anticipated the audiences' reaction. I was not disappointed. Their jumps, screams, and intense hand clasping was a credit to the filmmaker's skills. Knowing the story didn't stop me wanting to see the ending again, so I bounded down the dusty back fire escape, along the corridor and out through a disused air vent straight into the Circle.

Such a pity the young lady patron at that precise moment decided to reach for her handbag and placed her hand on me instead! As you can imagine it was as much a surprise for me as it was for her and those other patrons sitting around us. This unexpected scream resounded around the audience completely breaking the tension where there was not any intended. However, the audience soon stopped laughing, again spellbound by the race-against-time taking place on the screen.

I moved to a less noticeable position near the exit stairs to eagerly anticipate that final crashing cymbal. I sat there with my eyes glued to the screen, my whiskers like vibrating antennae, the fur on my back tingling, my tail wrapped firmly underneath me. Even though I had seen the film many times, I still took great delight in anticipating every familiar moment. Oh, how I hoped they hadn't changed the ending.

And then, without warning, a shot rang out that could be heard throughout the cinema.

They *had* changed the ending!

"You can't do that," I meowed in my loudest objective voice.

But still the movie continued towards its shattering climax. It took several moments and the sound of scuffling in the foyer before I realized that the gunshot we heard was not part of the movie.

Whilst the audience remained intrigued by the movie (and no doubt somewhat bewildered by the extraneous and unintentional gunshot 'on the soundtrack') I bounded down the stairs, across the Grand Circle foyer and peeped over the edge of the balcony.

A robbery was taking place at the ticket box, the culprit wielding a gun and tightly clutching a calico bag, no doubt filled with the day's takings. Outside the entrance could be heard the sound of sirens, and the screech of brakes. The thief's exit was blocked, so he bounded for the stairs, leaping them two at a time.

Running towards me I could see that he was a frightened young man, desperate to make his escape. I leapt from my hiding place beside the potted aspidistra plant, but he continued his frantic run, shouting abuse at me as he scurried past, and on into the Grand Circle foyer.

The foyer was deserted except for the Candy Bar staff who were finishing off restocking the bar from the hidden storage room in the corridor on the far side. The door was propped open and for the thief it was either up the stairs and into the cinema, or into the unknown through the open door. To his detriment he chose the latter.

The startled staff members were soon joining the chase into the corridors that led into the labyrinth behind and under the cinema. By now the manager was in close pursuit, shouting to the remaining staff to close the door behind him. And as for me, I raced back into the cinema, along the darkened aisle and back into the corridor via the disused air vent.

It was dark and cool inside this world, and I could hear muffled shouting for more torches. I deduced that not many of the staff even knew these passages existed, let alone knew their way around them. The thief knew even less. It was therefore up to me to track him down.

Beside me I could hear the ever-increasing orchestral crescendo coming through the speaker system. Ahead of me were the dark, cobwebbed corridors I loved to explore. And in the distance, the crashing sounds of the man as he stumbled across long forgotten memorabilia in the dark recesses.

It was like being an actor in my own movie. The score was being played, the plot was being enacted and in this exotic setting I was the star. As I bounded along through the gloom my body began to tingle with excitement.

I deduced that the thief would make his way from the first floor downwards towards the dressing rooms, no doubt hoping to find a suitable exit. He was going to be out of luck as all the wiring to that area had long ago disintegrated leaving nothing but total darkness. Another crashing sound reverberated along my corridor. Yes, my suspicions were correct. The sound came from my left, probably from the female dressing room. Our ability to see in the dark sometimes comes in very handy, and that night was one of those instances.

Down the stairs I bounded, my heart thumping with excitement. Around the corner past the stage manager's long-deserted office, under the rack of dusty, disused costumes and directly in to his path I went.

With a spine-tingling "M-E-O-W" that would have earned me an award for sound effects, he was 'caught' red handed by my night vision. I could see him but he couldn't see me.

He shouted abuse at me, but I had moved too quickly for him to locate me. As he stumbled about the dressing room in the dark his level of verbal aggression increased.

In the background I heard the crashing cymbal on the movie soundtrack bringing the story to its climax, and shortly thereafter the rustling of the audience as they began to leave the cinema.

Our thief had become quiet, deciding that he would hide until his escape was certain. The intermittent flash of torches could be seen at the far end of the corridor. Voices of staff members were joined by the gruffer and more aggressive police tones.

I could see the dusty cupboard that the thief had opted to hide in, so armed with this knowledge I bounded towards the flashing lights.

"Meow. Meow. Follow me. This way," I said.

The police officer in his rush to locate his quarry totally ignored me, but I persisted. My friend the cinema manager understood, and explained to the others that they should follow me downstairs.

The manager's torch highlighted the footprints in the dust made by the thief. No-one had traversed these corridors in years, so any intruder made an obvious mark. Down the stairs I bounded, the party in full pursuit, just like in that famous chase under the Paris Opera House.

To the bottom of the stairs, along the criss-crossed, cobwebbed corridor, past the faded star on the dressing room door and into the makeup area we went. The faded gilt mirrors reflected the urgency of the torches as they flashed to and fro. One could almost hear the hubbub and kafuffle of the dancing girls being interrupted as they prepared for another show.

I leapt past the rack of dresses and stood motionless in front of the cupboard marked MONSIEUR RODINE - Master Illusionist. Now they could capture their quarry.

"Stand back," said the senior police officer to the assembled group. "Come on out quietly. We have you surrounded," he shouted.

But there was no reply. He again shouted his warning to the thief - but still no response.

So, as quickly as a cat escapes a drenching, they surrounded the cupboard, and prized open the doors. Nothing - completely empty!

"Stupid cat!" shouted the officer, first looking at me and then glaring at my manager.

"Let's spread out. You take the rooms down there, you come with me."

My manager stayed with me. We both knew that the thief was close by and we would find him. But he couldn't be seen with my naked eye. I was mystified and perplexed, but my natural curiosity then led me into the cupboard to see for myself. Nothing - except for footprints in the dust! He had certainly been there, but how could he have disappeared so quickly?

But, wait, what was that? Was that a little sneeze? He's here somewhere behind this...

Suddenly, there was movement. My weight must have been enough to trigger the secret revolving door. As quick as a flash I found myself swirling in a half circle, plummeting into the darkness behind the back cavity.

As all this happened, I heard the manager shouting out, "He's here. Quick. Help me."

As I had been turned half circle into the darkness at the

back of the cupboard, so our thief had unexpectedly been caught off-guard and swung half-circle into the waiting hands of my manager. From my dark recess I could hear a scuffling and what sounded like the click of handcuffs being applied.

"What about me?" I meowed. But no one seemed to hear.

Now there were new voices. Voices that were asking questions about what had happened, was the money retrieved, how much was stolen?

Then, with not so much as a "howdy do", the platform swung me around into blinding light. My eyes took a moment to adjust, and then I saw the television news cameras. I was being beamed live across the country, the hero of the daring Bijou Cinema robbery.

My manager picked me up into his arms, brushed off the cobwebs and dust and carried me triumphantly up the stairs and into the foyer.

The biggest bowl of milk you have ever seen was waiting for me to enjoy. The news crews captured every moment of my reward, and eagerly took close-ups of me sitting contentedly beside my manager as he once again recounted the extraordinary events of that evening.

On rainy afternoons I sometimes like to sit with my master, the retired Bijou manager, and watch the video replays of those news services. "Was it me or wasn't it?" he asks, still very puzzled. I sit on the rug and purr contentedly knowing full well that "A Bijou Cat is (truly) a Happy Cat."

And as I smile inwardly, I know that there are some things a human just wouldn't understand!

Passing Over

We felines have no fear of death. As you may know, the saying "a cat has nine lives" is very much based on fact, the details closely observed by your ancestors over many generations.

We cats have come to this earth-plane as part of the journey that all spirit must undertake. The Ancient Gods, the creators of our souls, the givers of all wisdom, decided that they would make the act of death (or as some see it, the act of sleeping) our journey to the next level of consciousness. Such a test had to be undertaken by all. No human or creature would be immune from this act, nor could they stay on this earth-plane beyond their allotted years. All must advance their wisdom, or their spirit would return again to repeat their same earthly lessons rather than return as a more advanced soul.

With humans, it was found that they tended to enjoy life in the Garden of Eden, and when their allotted time span was drawing to a close, they panicked and decided that they really didn't want to go to the unknown. Over the generations this fear became hereditary and I understand, is still the greatest fear in the human mind. No escape! You must die sometime! The very thought seems to send humans into a frenzy of better diets, quitting smoking, beginning exercise routines and looking both ways *twice* before crossing the road. However, it has been my observation, that this frenzy of activity lasts only as long as to the next big social function, the next opportunity to abuse their earthly body. It is so sad that they do not realize they are spirit having an earthly experience and should therefore take better care of the body that encases them.

Now, we cats are very different from you humans (and how pleased I am to know that I will not be returning in another life as one of you). Back in *that* Garden in Eden, we felines were just another part of the animal hierarchy trying to survive from being eaten by bigger and more powerful creatures. Each day was just another day to exist, and so it was with relief that we died and our soul began its upward journey to enlightenment. We mostly lived our lives to the full, often taking chances, always seemingly oblivious to danger, always going with the flow of the natural universal laws. Of course, this was observed by humans, many of who thought that because of our nine lives that sometimes we were indestructible.

These thoughts whirled through my head as I sat taking the sun in the garden of a lovely colonial house that abutted that of my mistress' home. There was a delightful protected area of garden that I had claimed as my own, a little corner of the world that was continually bathed by the warm sun throughout the morning.

After the early morning playtime with my provider, and a delightful breakfast of cold milk and sardines, I frequently would bring myself here. In that isolated corner of heaven, undiscovered by human or feline, I could wash, snooze and generally let the world pass me by. From my little mound I could see all the comings and goings of that garden - the ladies in their smart white uniforms, Old Henry the gardener, leaning on his shovel as he enjoyed another hand-rolled cigarette, dignified middle-aged couples pacing the lawns in deep conversation, and the faces of those in the wheelchairs.

Some days I would stroll the grounds and take in the sights, and sounds, and smells at a closer proximity. As I walked among the occupants, my senses discovered a whole tapestry of delights. It was spring and the strong aroma of jasmine was carried on the drifts of warm air. Old Henry's tobacco was a powerful aroma too. As he bent down to stroke me, the pungent smell seemed to have even permeated his trousers to knee height.

From the open window of the main building wafted the aroma of freshly baked bread, that special aroma that seems to send humans into deep emotion as they react to childhood memories of mothers, and home cooking and gluttony. As always there was also the smell of perfume and talc and cheap bath-salts. As I ambled from person to person, so the intensity changed. The visiting couples usually had a different aroma for him and for her - hers being a light perfume, his, a heavy-handed splattering of a cheap essence no doubt designed to cover an array of natural body odors. The nurses offered merely a hint of perfume, whilst the women in their wheelchairs had that distinctive musty aroma that seems to permeate ladies of a mature age. My rule of paw with the latter, is that the stronger the perfume, the older the person.

It was therefore with great pleasure that I came across Mrs. Barnes, lightly perfumed, yet agreeably natural. My nose told me that we would become very good friends, though my heart ached with an unidentified sorrow and pain.

Whatever emotions my heart may have felt, on this glorious spring morning all I wanted to do was share the sheer joy of the day with a human I liked. My mistress would by now be at her work in the city, so, nothing ventured, nothing gained, I briskly trotted up to Mrs. Barnes. Seeing her sitting in her wheelchair, I gave her my friendliest "Meow" fully expecting a delighted face to respond to me and to reach down and pick me up for a cuddle. You must understand that this is not something that I do lightly or without some thought, so I was very perplexed at getting no response, except for a small flicker of recognition from her left eye. "Try again," I thought. But still there was no response.

"Oh, the poor dear," said a nearby nurse to a visiting couple. "She doesn't seem to want to respond to anything these days. She just sits. No talkies. No responses. No nothing."

And with that said, the nurse headed towards the big house leaving the lady of the couple to burst into tears.

"Meow." "Meow." Had I lost my power of persuasion?

Surely not!

It was then that the tearful lady noticed me. Perhaps it was because by then I had pulled out the big guns. Deep-pool eyes looking mournfully skyward generally does the trick, and today was going to be no exception. She gently bent down, stroked me with a hand that was used to caressing beautiful objects and slowly lifted me up into the folds of her arms. Her clothing was of the softest cotton, with just a whiff of an exquisite perfume. As she held me close to her body I could feel a wonderful sense of caring and trust.

And as she gently stroked me she spoke to the gentleman about how much her mother loved cats, and with the gentleness of a mother handling her new born babe for the first time, she placed me on the old lady's lap.

It was very comfortable to be sitting in the warmth of the mid-morning sun. To feel the body warmth from the old lady, to feel an immediate emotional attachment to her and her visiting daughter – this was sheer bliss for me.

The daughter bent down to stroke me again, whispering in my ear...

"This is my mother, Mrs. Barnes. Please give her your love and stay with her awhile. It would mean so much to her."

And with that she turned and walked with the gentleman towards the big house.

And so, in this beautiful corner of the garden, Mrs. Barnes

and I just sat together soaking up the pleasant warm sunshine. We spoke no common language. Neither of us wanted to move, and neither of us wanted this moment to end.

I must have drifted off to sleep for a period, for I was not aware of when her finger had begun to caress my ear. As I drifted back to consciousness I felt an overwhelming sensation of contentment, a contentment that had become deliciously entangled with an all-over tingling feeling. Mrs. Barnes, it seemed, was coming back to life.

It was just a little movement at first, a mere finger stroke along the ear. And then a tentative movement along my nose, over the eyes, culminating in an open palm stroking my head. This is something a cat like myself just simply cannot resist.

And soon I was purring away as if there was no tomorrow. Sometimes I do believe that we have moments in time that equate to what Heaven is like. And this was one of those moments. Sunshine. Warmth. Love. Contentment. A combination that says I am at one with the universe.

I slowly turned my head and gazed upward towards Mrs. Barnes' face. As I rolled onto my back I was able to absorb at once the lifetime of care and anguish that this face had recorded. It was soft, with a gentleness that spoke of love and caring. Even the wrinkles seemed to flow in channels of beauty. Her eyes were now deep reservoirs of calm, and her lips, a faded pink like a late summer rose. It was as if all the cares and strife that accompany life's journey were now held at bay. Her eyes, and no doubt her heart, simply stated that they had had enough.

Mrs. Barnes was, at that exquisite moment, between two worlds. No longer interested in the earthly but not yet clearly seeing the hereafter. For just a wee time, she was waiting.

We cats do have a sixth sense, and we do know how to look into the heart and recognize the truth. Mrs. Barnes was dying, and up to this point, seemingly alone. But the slow stroking finger told me that she was grateful for my being there. This was a journey that could be shared and made easier by having a loving companion. It was now clear that it was my immediate destiny to be there to assist in her journey.

"Sister, why is that cat sitting on Mrs. Barnes' knee?" shouted a voice from the middle of the lawn. "Get it off her immediately!"

A rush of white clad nursing staff descended towards me intent on dispatching me to other parts.

I was caught so unawares by this action that I didn't have time to move. Suddenly and without warning, the gaggle of white stopped motionless in their tracks. With one hand firmly on my back, and the other slowly raised in defiance, Mrs. Barnes whispered out loud "Stop! She is my friend, and you will not touch her!"

As if the Apocalypse had happened before their very eyes, they froze in mid-flight.

"But Mrs. Barnes... you can talk!" came a shocked retort.

"Why, of course I can," she gently replied, giving a little grin. Looking down at my bemused face, and with a twinkle in her eye, she whispered to me how grateful she was to have me as a friend.

And so it was, over the remainder of the spring and into early summer that I spent many happy hours with my new friend. The nurse would wheel her out of the hostel into the sunshine, and I would come to visit as frequently as I could. Often we would just sit, the two of us, soaking up the warm sun, quietly contemplating the beauty of the gardens and the importance of friendship.

One day, in high summer, my companion failed to rendezvous with me at our special corner of the garden. The nursing staff seemed busy with the other patients, caring little for a cat who had taken up morning residence with them. Perturbed by this mysterious event, I went in search of Mrs. Barnes.

Across the lawns, around the sunflowers and down past the azaleas I scampered. Being a curious cat I had long ago discovered where my friend went to rest when she was taken back into the house.

On that particular morning I could see that her ground floor window was ajar, the curtains flapping idly in the warm breeze that blew the scent of honeysuckle across the flowerbeds.

With a precise leap I was soon on the windowsill peering inside. There was my friend lying in bed peacefully asleep, whilst to the other side of the room there was a forest of equipment that had obviously been recently in use. There was no one else in the room, so I gave my usual friendly "meow" to say that I was there. One eye slowly stirred, and into the room I leapt. In a single bound I was on the bed, soon snuggling close to my friend.

As one 'knows' that danger lurks, so on this day I instinctively 'knew' that my friend's spirit would be leaving this world. Around her was an aura of tranquility, a warm blue light of peace and contentment. On this day a soul would slip silently from its mortal body and cross that threshold of light to continue its journey. It has been my observation that people who know they are going to die prefer to do so when friends and family are nearby, but just out of sight. Quietly and silently, the soul departs.

And so it was that Mrs. Barnes passed away that morning, her hand upon my back, a smile upon her lips with the only sound, apart from my purring, being the monotonous ticking of the bedside clock. A peaceful passing achieved - the ultimate goal for all of us.

Now as I sit here in the warm sunshine of my little corner of the garden, I have mixed feelings - happiness that the passing of Mrs. Barnes was a peaceful one for her. Sadness, that no human could be regarded as her friend to the end, to be by her side, to hold her hand. We cats have a wonderful gift - we have the gift of time. We can spend all the time in the world with our family, our providers, the other human friends we choose. Yet time to care, and time to share, seems such a rare commodity in *your* world.

At least on this beautiful morning, I shall sleep contented knowing that my friend's journey was made just a little easier because I gave of my time.

Klaus, the Hero Cat

As I sit here in the warm sun the expression "I have dreamed a dream" looms large in my mind. I don't quite know why, but perhaps it has something to do with hope. I am reminded of a story that has been handed down from father to son in our lineage, a story that shows that the oppressed, the frightened and the very smallest all seek that same universal dream of freedom. And how important it is, no matter your size, to give with a full and loving heart to what you believe in.

It is said that Klaus will live forever as a symbol of courage in the tiny town of Yarbourg, and that the statue of him in the square will remind everyone who sees it, that freedom is precious.

Klaus was the last kitten born in a litter of nine, and as often happens, was the smallest and the weakest. The country barn was at least warm, his mother's milk satisfying and the straw on which he lay had the delicious aroma of being recently cut. His very earliest memories, before his eyes had opened, were of these barnyard aromas and the associated noises. He couldn't individually distinguish them, but in his mind they helped identify his location.

Sometimes there would be a sudden noise of a heavy door-bolt slamming open, and the cold wind would enter his world. The human voices were full of anger and hate, and there was often a great deal of shouting. And always, in the distance, there was the sound of what I came to know as gunfire. For a blind kitten in a strange new world, day and night were the same. But as clear sight slowly came to him, he discovered that his home was high up in a barn, on a ledge of straw that allowed he and his brothers and sisters to look down on everything in the building. Being the youngest and weakest, he was the first to be pushed aside by his siblings when it came to seeking his mother's milk.

Soon he became very hungry and began to cry.

He tried to walk along the ledge, but his little legs were too weak to hold him. In an instant he had toppled over the side, landing in a very undignified position in the straw beside the startled horse, and near to where the cow was quietly chewing her cud. To his surprise and delight, near the cow were little white puddles of her milk, the first extractions before the milk for the family was put into the bucket. In the wink of an eye he was again feeling the sheer delight of milk caressing his palate. And in two winks of an eye, he was sound asleep on the straw near the cow.

The bomb that exploded on the barn that night, and the subsequent fire, should have killed him. He awoke with the sound of the bomb's detonation ringing in his ears, and the sight of flames all around him. Panic-stricken human voices could be heard above the crackling flames, and all around him was a scene like the fires of hell.

How he escaped the inferno remains a mystery, but the morning after, he was a very burnt, sore and hungry kitten. As he sat huddled in the cool grass watching the smoke rise from the charred remains of the barn, all he could do was whimper a call to the world. Two weeks old, much of his fur singed from his skin, his paws all black and burnt, his family dead, his stomach tight with hunger. There he was, alone in a world gone mad with hate. Why was he still alive? What was to become of him? He didn't know.

So, on that cold winter morning in 1941, on a lonely farm, on a European mountainside, he cried himself to sleep.

But to all those who believe it so, there truly is a god. And for those who have forgotten, or have rejected, or are simply too young to know, this god of peace still comes to even the most lowly and miserable of his creatures and helps them in their time of need. And so it was that day that the god worked his mercy through a little girl.

As Anna stood with her parents looking at the remains of the family barn, she looked across the grass and saw Klaus. Her hands were warm and gentle as she slowly stroked the kitten's head.

It was not long before Klaus re-awoke to find himself inside a kitchen. He was being held in a soft, warm blanket in the arms of the little girl. Her eyes were innocent and caring, and without a word spoken, Klaus knew that here was a friend, someone who cared. Her mother was fussing about, warming some milk, and then testing it on her wrist to check on the temperature. Through an eyedropper the warm, soothing milk was soon entering Klaus' little mouth. He was weak and confused, but somehow he felt contented with this family. He decided there and then he would adopt them as his own.

Over the next few weeks Klaus was surrounded by love and attention. He was allowed to sleep on his blanket beside the wood-fired stove, and, imperceptibly at first, his fur began to grow back, so that by the arrival of spring he looked like any other cat of his age. He had a bounce in his step, his fur was full and sleek, his appetite was good and he had the most wonderful playmate in Anna. And it was she who called him Klaus, after her favorite uncle who had died in the war.

Spring was a lovely time on the farm. The air was warm, flowers filled the fields on the hillsides and the sky was blue like an endless lake. Anna and Klaus would romp in the fields, running and jumping, and rolling around for hours on end. They would have little picnics near the stream. Anna would take bread and cheese for herself, as well as a little container of milk for Klaus. And, at the end of the day they would cuddle up tightly together in Anna's bed, fall asleep and dream of the childhood joy of always being free, of being able to do exactly what they pleased. They were a few deliriously happy weeks they would both remember.

Unfortunately in reality, they weren't free. Certainly, Anna had the freedom from responsibility and care that all children have when they are young, but she lived in a world where the adults were angry. Where one's love of a country meant dying for it. Where men in black shiny boots with red spiders on their shirts precision marched through the villages. And where machines choked the fresh air with explosions of fire and smoke. It was a time where just to stay alive was a daily chore. Men's voices rang through the air - sharp, arrogant, pitiless. And this was a world where animals merely existed, found food wherever and whenever they could, and were seen to be part of the human food chain whenever it was expedient.

On the farm Anna and Klaus were only occasionally aware of this outside world. The burning of the barn had been a stark reminder of how quickly their world could change.

And on that night in May it changed forever. Anna and Klaus were already snuggled up in bed when they became aware of the marching feet on the gravel road leading to the farmhouse. The knocking on the door became very intense. Father called out that he was coming, and mother had rushed to Anna's room to console her.

Downstairs there was a great deal of shouting, and soon a man in the black uniform stood in Anna's bedroom doorway shouting at Anna and her mother. They were terrified as they followed orders to get dressed and move downstairs. The uniformed man reached forward to grab Klaus by the scruff of the neck. Klaus reacted instinctively, scratching the soldier across the back of his wrist. The soldier shouted an obscenity, reached for his pistol and endeavored to shoot Klaus. Anna's kicking and jostling of the soldier sent the bullet smashing through the bedroom window. Klaus scurried across the bedcovers, through the soldier's legs and out into the main part of the house.

There was much shouting and abuse from all participants, before everyone departed. Anna and her parents were marched at gunpoint out of the house and loaded onto a truck. Nearby the soldiers talked about the village and the train that would pass through it the next evening. With the soldiers there was a good deal of merriment, but on the trucks there was silence and gloom.

Klaus observed all of these happenings from the half open attic window, his eyes and ears wide open. He now had a very distinct disliking of these men in black uniforms and was determined to discover what was happening to his beloved Anna.

Down through the darkened house he bounded and out into the night. He was determined to follow the soldiers and the trucks along the road that led down into the village. Somewhere down there he would find his Anna.

All through that night he ran and jumped and walked the road, sometimes skirting past the little groups of soldiers who were smoking and drinking on the roadside, sometimes crossing the fields of wildflowers, and taking the shortcuts alongside the swiftly flowing stream. By morning, he was nearing the edge of the village. He could hear the sounds of the church bell that now called the villagers to work rather than the faithful to prayer. And he could see the villagers beginning their trek to the work camp. He could sense the feeling of spirits that were repressed, of lives where the sunshine no longer shone, and hearts that were heavy with a burden of the great unknown. To see the futility of war, all one has to do is look into the eyes and hearts of its innocent victims. When, oh when, will men give up these silly pursuits, he reflected to himself.

Across the other side of the railway tracks, and just up the hill, he could see a lot of activity. From the long wooden huts sleepy people were being shouted and cajoled into starting their day. He deduced that this was some sort of camp where people were held, then marched through the town and loaded onto trains. The camp had many trucks, and so it was in this direction Klaus headed in search of his beloved Anna.

Barbed wire may be a deterrent to human access, but not so for a cat, (although it is true that caution had to be taken as he wound his way through the lethal spirals.)

The camp was bustling with activity and no one had time to notice the presence of one small cat. Klaus was therefore able to move from hut to hut without impediment. Windows were few in number, but low enough for him to leap onto the ledge and look inside. Hut after hut gave him disappointment - so many sad faces, so much anxiety and so many tears.

It was not until mid-morning that he finally saw Anna. Clutching her favorite rag doll that she had managed to grab as she was taken from her house, she sat on the bare ground, part of a large group awaiting instructions. On padded paw Klaus moved quickly and silently to the back of the group, beginning his trek towards Anna. As he moved past arms and elbows and silent seated bodies, he was patted and caressed with a love that he had not previously known from strangers. They were emotional caresses, as of parents to children, who were giving their offspring a final farewell, knowing that they were not to meet again. It was like a spiritual passing on of wisdom from one generation to another, the passing of the torch of life to another to carry it on in their imminent absence.

And there ahead was Anna, her back to him, her sobbing carried on the wind. He paused to savor that moment when the impossible can become a reality, when 'lost' souls come home. He gave a soft "Meow" and walked forward to nuzzle under her arm. He was again at peace.

On that morning, sitting together, there was perfect harmony between Anna and Klaus. A delicious melding of two pure hearts, of two souls together in a moment of time, both savoring the company of the other and both knowing deep within their hearts that such joy could not last.

The arrival of the black uniformed man, with the fresh scar on his wrist soon put an end to their moment. Klaus was quickly hidden under a jacket and told not to move or make a noise. He understood. Cats do understand human talk, and on that morning Klaus heard it all.

"No food today."

"The separation of men, women and children."

"A march through the village in the early evening."

"The boarding of the train to take them to another country."

When the uniformed man had finished shouting his orders, and departed to dictate them to yet another group of detainees, the atmosphere of Anna's group became different. The men talked of escape and rioting, the mothers held their children tightly to their bosom and the single women sat with the quiet stoicism of martyrdom.

Klaus sat quietly on Anna's lap wondering what he could do to help. He was just a lone cat in a large human world, though surely there was something he could do for Anna and her family?

As he watched the sad faces around him, his mind glimmered a germ of an idea.

He then gave Anna a special purr, licked her face, nudged her cheek.... and was gone.

A series of hands and disturbed voices tried to stop him leaving, but before you could say "auf wiedersehen" he was out of the camp and running down towards the village.

In the distance he could hear the express trains roaring through the station carrying arms, or soldiers or other human cargo. "Trains of death," he whispered angrily to no-one in particular.

Soon he found himself near the railway tracks. Somehow he would have to use his cunning against the might of the human war machine. And do it quickly. He reasoned that without the trains, his Anna and her family couldn't be taken from the village to suffer whatever injustice might be planned for them.

As he prowled alongside the many tracks that ran side by side he observed that they all passed a control box near the station before crossing a bridge at the edge of the village. Along the station platform he walked, looking for what, he knew not. Then it was across the tracks to the signal box.

The door was open and in he slinked - up the stairs and into the heart of the control area. The elderly villager was too pre-occupied with studying timetables to notice Klaus. Around him were levers and lights of all descriptions. This was obviously a very important part of the railway. Maybe even the heart of it, he thought to himself. And so a glimmer of an idea began to grow in Klaus' mind. Destroy the signal box, and no more trains could come or go for some considerable time. But how - how?

The old man momentarily looked away from reading his piles of schedules, and it was only then that he noticed Klaus. Bending down, he swept Klaus into the air and made him welcome, placing him on the scheduling ledge where he could look out and see the entire railway layout. "Yes," said

Klaus to himself, "destroy this signal box and all would be saved."

The man lit up his pipe, prepared the little wood-fired stove to cook his meal and shared a tidbit of meat with Klaus. Klaus suddenly realized how hungry and tired he was.

It was the unannounced crackling of the radio bursting into life that woke him. It was already late afternoon and where was he? The sharp, gruff, military voice was dictating details to the old man about the special trains for that evening, including the empty train coming to collect the prisoners, as well as the many freight trains carrying warheads to the front. In the background Klaus could hear the clipped sounds of soldiers marching on cobblestones, and what was more disturbing, the muffled sounds of scores of other feet as they shuffled and walked through the village.

Gathering his senses, he knew that he had to work fast. Looking around, he saw that the signal-master had been disturbed from tending his fire by the urgency of the radio message. The door of the firebox was still open, the fire inside beginning to take hold, the old man pre-occupied with the scheduling details.

From his perch on the desk beside the pile of disheveled papers Klaus was startled by the unexpected train whistle just outside the box. As the express roared through the station his body swung around in surprise. The papers went sprawling in all directions. The signal-master spun around to see all hell breaking loose.

The papers that fell near the open firebox had quickly ignited, spreading flames across the littered floor like a forest fire. This was no place for man or cat. Klaus had already made a dash for the stairs, and the signal-master wasn't far behind. The whole building was a tinderbox, and it quickly became apparent that, by accident or design, it was now a raging inferno and would soon burn to the ground.

Klaus knew fire all too well from his kitten-hood, and the smell of singed fur and thick black smoke made him nauseous. The searing pain in his eyes from the falling timber joist made his escape seem impossible. He couldn't see where to go and the pain was excruciating.

The signalman saw Klaus' dilemma. And with a grand sweep of his arm picked him up by the scruff of the neck and carried him to safety inside his rugged military coat.

As the two occupants fled into the evening light, soldiers came running from all directions, many being ordered to leave the marching prisoners to help fight the fire. Above all the shouting, the orders and the abuse came the sound of another express train, it's whistle whining an eerie doomsday call through the night sky.

The ferocity of the two military transport trains exploding on impact was heard right across the valley. A huge column of fiery light lit the evening sky as the thunderous scraping of heavy metal seared through the heart of soldier, prisoner, villager, and cat.

Panic was everywhere in the village. No one knew what was going on, or where the attack had emanated. Was this the beginning of the much-promised liberation?

Amidst all this mayhem, in a side street of the village, two adults and a little girl could be seen moving swiftly and silently towards the darkened countryside, three escapees fleeing to a new life somewhere beyond the mountains that they loved so much. Elsewhere in the village a lonely and frightened old man carried his new feline friend away from the furore, as together they too sought refuge in the darkness of the countryside.

It took another three years before peace again mantled this alpine village in tranquility and harmony.

It was a warm, early summer's day as the old man sat on his balcony reading the headline in the re-established local newspaper....

"CAT CAUSED CATASTROPHE!

Hero's story can now be told!"

Smiling from ear to ear, he read aloud the story to his feline companion. There it was, just as he had told the reporter, how *his* cat had saved over 500 prisoners and had caused havoc on the transport of the soldiers and their deadly cargoes. Klaus smiled inwardly and drifted off to sleep.

"Excuse me, Sir," said the female voice. "May I pat your cat? He looks so much like a cat that I once owned. His name was Klaus, and together we shared many happy times."

And with his approval she reached down and gently began to stroke the fur.

"Anna," thought Klaus, "is it really you?"

Instinctively he knew it was, and he purred and "meowed" in response.

"Like so many in the Great War, he was a casualty," said the old man. "He was blinded as a result of the great fire, and I am now his eyes. And yes, he is a hero to this village."

Anna was filled with tears as she gave Klaus a hug.

"Thank you my brave friend. Your love and devotion has not been forgotten during all these years. My mother and my father and I will always be in your debt and you will always be in my heart. I am going to live in the city now, and so my friend, this must be good-bye. May the great god of peace bless you and keep you safe."

And with that, her eyes overflowing with tears, Anna left to begin her new life in the city.

In due course, and after several seasons, the old man died. Anna could not be contacted, now lost in a city where neighbors do not know each other and childhood family friendships become discarded.

But on a snowy, winter's day as Anna walked alone in the city park, she heard the church bells slowly peeling for a funeral. In her heart she instinctively knew that Klaus had also died that day. When hearts are filled with love, then distance, time and lack of contact are no barriers.

And, as her heart had said, so it was.

Not long after, Anna returned to the village, quietly and without anyone's knowledge. There she placed a wildflower at the base of Klaus' newly erected statue. And as a tear rolled from her cheek and onto the flower she read the plaque that accompanied the statue -

On velvet paws he moved

through every heart he met

A love so pure

That none of us will 'er forget

A Borgia-style Cocktail

The late afternoon air was crackling with the thrusts of lightning bolts. The atmosphere rumbled with the sound of rolling thunder. The rain was just beginning to fall. This was not the place for a cat to be. But it was *the* place to be if you were setting about executing the perfect crime of murder!

Why was I there in that country villa, sitting on that stone fence looking through the open window of the gardening shed at a young man intently working at a bench? As well as the electricity that permeated this delicious warm summer atmosphere, (an electricity that had my fur standing on end), there was a definite aroma of deadly intent being carried on the wind. The wind, warm and caressing as only that of late summer can bring, also included the sweetness of blossoms from all the surrounding gardens occupied by the wealthy and their entourages.

My mistress had spent the summer in the company of one James Kirkwood, financier, art collector, and multi-millionaire and now she was with him on his island retreat. But, it is I who has benefited the most from her travels. As partners in life's journey, she has treated me in the luxurious manner that befits the long tradition we felines have for centuries aspired to.

The private jet was so much better than many of my previous traveling experiences in cramped, dark, aircraft holds, manhandled by persons of obnoxious habits, strange aromas, foreign accents and no affinity with the special needs that we feline aristocrats require. And thanks to the Gods of Ra, for on this trip, no injections were required.

How civilized it was, to be carried on board our very own jet, allowed to roam the aisles and cockpit at will, scratch at the carpet, and fall asleep to the gentle sounds of champagne glasses tinkling their merriment. And how quaint a human custom it is to perform the latter, touching glasses of bubbly and wishing good things to the other drinkers. Can you imagine moi pushing my milk bowl towards a fellow feline, clinking the two containers and meowing sweetly "Here's to many happy days ahead" or "Cheers! To many more happy divorces!" No, I think not!

We cats have nothing to worry about so long as we have you humans doing all the worrying and working for us. Our place in the pecking order is to simply be ourselves, be totally looked after, be indulged and pampered, and to sleep as often and as frequently as we can. As long as we have you under our spell, our life is very contented.

Of course, there are humans who have canine instincts, and James was one of them. Sadly, they bring discord and upheaval into the lives of the opposite persuasion, the feline.

According to my observations, the world seems divided into

two groups - the Canines: aggressive, athletic, self-centered, odorous (yuk, who needs doggy smells!), gregarious, emotionally incomplete and very territorial. And us, the adorable Felines: languorous, contented, emotionally complete, clean, and devoted (purr, purr). Of course, there are a few people of neither persuasion; they and their diverse animal companions are of no consequence here.

In common language, James hated cats. But he was a smart enough canine human to know that the way to my mistress' heart was through me. The moment we met, my skin was repulsed. It took no effort to show my displeasure by standing my fur on end. "Nice kitty. Nice kitty" comments were not going to wash with this cat! James and I had it in for each other from the very beginning.

Whenever I was within sight of my mistress he made overtures to be friendly to me. This of course, allowed me to control the situation. I claimed for myself the luxurious flock rug that was strewn centre stage, in front of the fire. I sat on his expensive tapestry cushions, drank and ate from silver bowls and even allowed myself the indulgent bedevilment of sitting on *his* knee whilst sinking my claws ever deeper into his flesh knowing full well that he dare not accuse moi of causing mischief or pain. Strolling poolside the next day, I noticed that a discreet patch of sticking plaster just below his swimming trunks proved adequate testimony to my evil deed.

"Don't mess with we felines!" I purred aggressively as I jumped one limb higher in the olive tree.

From there I was protected from the hot Mediterranean sun as well as having a commanding view of the house, the swimming pool and the extensive gardens that contoured right through to the stone fence near the potting shed at the back of the property.

Sleep overcame me very quickly, and soon I was mixing dreams of Genghis Cat, Pied Piper Pussy and moi, leading a mighty army of feline warriors, scourging the world of dogs and all those attracted to them. Carried aloft by four devoted humans, resting on my pillow of plush velvet and gold braid, I commanded my troops.

"Bring me their heads.... and bring me my milk!" I demanded. "Immediately!" Oh, the bliss of having so many servants devoted entirely to making one happy instead of having to make do with just one mistress. Dreams are such satisfaction to the soul!

I was still in this dream when the hushed sounds of men talking beneath my tree awakened me.

"We can't take any chances. She must have seen the handover and realized what you were doing. She mustn't be allowed to get to the police or tell anyone else about us. You have got to eliminate her without causing any suspicion. And it's got to be done pronto. Don't let her leave the villa for any reason."

"I'll do it as quickly as possible," replied the second voice.

With one very drowsy eye open I peered down.

"James!" I exclaimed with a loud purr. He must have heard me, for a sharp, teeth-clenched reply pierced the air in my direction.

"And you, my furry fuzzball, you will die with her. Fizzzzzz!" he fumed through clenched teeth.

As you can imagine I was by now wide-awake. I have been called a lot of things in my life, but "fuzzball" was going too far over the top. With the memory of my exalted dream status still pounding in my brain, this meant action. This meant WAR!

The two men moved away. The former drove off in his expensive red sports car, whilst the resident enemy moved inside the villa.

With agility that I quite surprised myself that I had within me, I bounded down the trunk, across the sundeck and in through the open French doors. The sound of muted conversation came from the lounge area in the room beyond. I silently moved forward to listen.

"Darling, let's make tonight a special one with just the two of us here, alone, in the villa. And it's my treat to make dinner. I'll make your favorites, and I'll find a special wine from the cellar."

"Oh, darling, that would be wonderful."

"You go to your room and rest, and leave everything to me. Shall we say eight o'clock? I'll come and fetch you, just like on our first date."

"Mmmmm. Yes please," she moaned back in blissful anticipated pleasure.

Nausea is not a state that a cat likes to be in, but listening to that slimy man talking was like having a fur-ball. You hate it being there, and so pleased when it's been dispatched. James had that exact same effect on me. He was up to no good, and my mistress and I were both clearly in his deadly sights.

As she wended her way up the stairs, he quietly slipped into the rambling country kitchen and began the preparation. James was normally a conservative man, not prone to showing much emotion, but on this particular afternoon he was positively aglow with feelings. Skipping from job to job he hummed and sang his favorite songs, including one I recognized about a Mr. Sweeny Todd, who in old London town made delicious pies from freshly killed human prey (and, heaven forbid, maybe from cats as well).

By late afternoon we both found ourselves at the potting shed at the back of the garden. There I was, sitting crouched on the stone fence watching him mix a potion of garden insecticides, weed killer and cabbage moth dust. Outside, lightning was regularly piercing the sky. Thunderclouds were beginning to open their reservoirs and there I was getting drenched to the skin, watching this contemporary scene from Macbeth being acted out in front of me.

In time the deadly cocktail was produced, siphoned into the

waiting wine bottle, corked and with a generous layer of dust and cobweb from the shed floor added to the outside to make it authentically vintage. The murderous scenario was ready to be enacted.

Back in the house he had closed all the doors and windows to keep out the storm. Unfortunately that also excluded me from taking part in his little passion play. As I peered in through the rain-lashed doors, I could hear the clock strike eight o'clock. "Showtime," I thought, and right on cue, into the dining room they came, arm in arm. The wind and rain in my ears made it impossible to hear the ensuing conversation, but after the starter course had been eaten I could see him produce *the* bottle of wine. With a suave gesture he showed her the label, she nodded approval and it was opened and left on the table to breathe.

What could I do to stop this dreadful act from taking place? My body was wet and bedraggled, but my mind was alert. I needed to get to that bottle and somehow destroy it. I needed to get inside the house.

Around to the kitchen window I went. But neither of the occupants looked up at me. What to do? "My tail, my tail. Use the tail to hit the window," I thought. The fur was heavy with moisture, so gathering all my strength, I flung it against the closed windowpane with all my might.

The attention I got was instantaneous, the breaking of the glass being the clincher.

My mistress came running to my aid, whilst he shrieked and

shouted about leaving the wet bastard outside. She won, of course, and the feeling of the warm kitchen towel caressing my soaked fur was bliss. Naturally he stared daggers at me, but with the innate staring ability found in all cats, he soon had to turn his eyes away.

"Let's have some wine," he shouted. And went in to the dining room to pour two glasses of red wine. No doubt one for himself from an untainted bottle and one for my mistress from the deadly cocktail!

He returned, giving one to her, and holding the other in his hand. She was still drying me, when the phone rang. Leaving the two glasses side by side on the kitchen bench, he went to answer it, and was soon in deep conversation with the caller.

As luck would have it, my wet fur required a second towel, so off my mistress went up the stairs to the linen cupboard near the back bedroom. I was alone for a few precious seconds, so what would you have done in my stead?

Exactly! But how was I to do it?

The bench was quite high, but a leap onto the kitchen chair, and up onto the bench would do it. At the time of a life-threatening decision, adrenalin is copiously released, even in a cat, so it was with astounding agility that I reached the bench top and found the two glasses of wine side by side. We cats do learn by osmosis the habits of humans, and in times of crisis like this one, such habits can be useful. With a gentle nudge or two from a nose, combined with a paw to stabilize, it is surprising how easily a glass of wine can be, shall we say, re-located.

Of course, my mistress did have some explaining to do to the police, but the mind-altering substances and the inordinately large amounts of cash found posthumously in the clothing and strong box of the said James Kirkwood, soon cleared her of any wrong doing.

With no urgency to leave during the protracted police investigation, the remaining weeks of summer were spent at the villa in quiet satisfaction, just my mistress and I, the warming breezes of lazy summer afternoons caressing our bodies whilst we both drank our respective containers of delicious cold milk.

Wine was decidedly off the menu!

Temple Cat

This beautiful Asian island is known throughout the world for its lush vegetation, sparkling white beaches and its gentle spiritual people.

There is warmth to be found here, not just of climatic atmosphere but also of the human heart. You awake in the mornings with an internal purity of spirit, and a world seemingly cleansed of its wrong doings.

The pre-dawn evokes a calmness of the soul that is at the one time both magical and timeless. The night air has warmth that does not invite the addition of bedclothes or night attire. As one lies in that twilight time when the mind is at its most fanciful, the sounds of the sea can be heard in the distance as it endlessly and rhythmically rolls and breaks on the nearby beach, the gentle tinkling of the wind-chimes dancing on the night breezes and the flickering of the candle in the corner of the room.

Here on the ridge, sited above the lush tropical vegetation and the village, was the ancient Temple of a Thousand Seasons, a place of worship so old that its apt name had borne witness to scores of generations of pilgrims seeking spiritual guidance for their earthly journey.

As usual in this season, there had been the overnight rain. But now, just after dawn, the gentle warm breezes were beginning to meander their way through the treetops. The dark rain clouds in the leaden sky were beginning to break up, and there remained a dull, heaviness in the air around the Temple. The early morning call of the birds announcing the dawn could be heard, and their low flying skimming across the grass was the first sign of activity for the day. The first rays of sunrise gave the landscape a veneer of somber color, a hue that lacked the brightness that only sunshine can give. The perfumes from the many vibrant flowers were only just becoming heady to his nostrils. There was the silence associated with sleep and lack of human activity. On the horizon, an iridescent glow that offered the promise of another sunny day in paradise.

And so it was that Mamat, the temple cat, could be seen lethargically moving around the village gardens. He observed the open-sided houses with their curtains aimlessly moving in the early morning breeze, the flickering candles losing their fight against the emerging morning. The black silhouetted tree-trunks of the banyan trees, still damp and foreboding standing strong and steady like living statues. The chickens clucked and scratched their way into the soft chocolate-colored soil seeking that elusive first worm of the day.

Mamat was making his way to the home of Wayan, his special human friend, who lived on the other side of a patch of trees. Shallow pools of fresh rainwater lay undisturbed along the un-made forest track. The creeper entangling the dead tree trunk dripped the last of the pre-dawn droplets to the grass below. And ahead of him as he emerged from the forest, were the feverishly squawking ducks. Eager to catch the early morning insects they impatiently awaited their master's arrival to herd them into the nearby flooded paddy fields.

"Come Wayun. Let's go. The insects are waiting," their impatient squawks seemed to call.

Necks erect, heads held high as if peering over an invisible object, they waited, dancing their impatience like firewalkers on hot coals, with eyes eternally searching for any sign of their human leader.

Yet, still audible above this scene, could be heard the tinkling of the ever-present wind chimes - the time honored link between man and his gods. As the chimes dangle in space, they have a freedom and voice that is unique. To many spiritual believers they represent a halfway house, a royal telephone that allows the gods to communicate with us all. The heavenly breezes, as were present on that morning, moved gently through the bamboo pipes. Their soft, eerie murmurings, and gentle touching of one another, sent a sound of peace and tranquility to the surrounding world. To be gently awoken by the sounds of the gods whispering sacred sounds to your ear is to begin your day in heavenly peace and harmony. "Move gently through this new day. Give of your love to all you meet. Respect all life you encounter. Give generously of your smile. Give of your time as thanks for this new day."

And so the new day had begun.

Wayan, the first-born of his family and hence his traditional name, emerged from his bamboo home, his eyes still bleary from sleep. Although he had been following this same routine for most of his 24 years, he still found it difficult to start his day with very much energy. That is where I come in.

For several years now I have been making my way each morning from the Temple, down through the village to Wayan's house, then spending the morning shepherding the ducks before I return during the heat of the day to the coolness of the Temple and to my duties there. Wayan is dressed in white T-shirt, red coolie hat, thongs and his batik working sarong. Oh, how I love my morning brush with the fringe at the bottom of that sarong. Delicious shivers delight my whole body, awakening me from my nocturnal state and reminding me that this is a new day.

Those pesky ducks and their persistent squawking soon brought me back to reality, so as the first golden rays of sunshine permeated the morning air, Wayan, myself and 23 gangly, waddling and highly excited ducks set forth towards the paddy fields.

To get to the flooded area we needed to travel along a patchwork of mounds that divided the fields. Mostly we use single file, Wayan leading the ducks like a Pied Piper with his 'children' in tow, with me running and scampering around encouraging any wayward bodies to keep up with the group. In other areas we are a group. These ducks know no other master, Wayan being the first life that they saw when their eyes opened. Consequently they will follow him anywhere. My role is to be an assistant, but more importantly as friend and confidant to Wayan. He saved my life when I was a tiny kitten, and so each day I repay his kindness with help and companionship.

Today will not be a long one in the fields as it is Festival Day, one of many held throughout the year at my Temple. Whilst the ducks are feeding on the insects, Wayan talks to me about his forthcoming trip to the city, the first he will make there since a brief visit when he was a little boy.

"Ah, my little friend, I must journey to meet with the men who hold the important papers about my land. My father told me that when he died this land would remain with me so that when I marry I will be able to continue to live on my own little part of the world just as my ancestors have done for all the generations before me. And soon I will ask Ni Ketut to be my wife."

In the warm morning sun we sat and talked. Wayan talked about his hopes and dreams, and I listened and purred back my loving response. Little did either of us know what else the gods had planned for us that day?

When the sun was high in the sky we all meandered our way back to the village.

The scene on our return was one of last minute hustle as offerings to the gods were in the final stages of preparations. The women had prepared huge compilations of fruits meticulously arranged on plates until they were several feet high. Layer upon layer of color, in ever decreasing circles of enticement made you wonder how these could ever be transported on the heads of the women. The gods had been abundant that season, and so it was that they should be worshipped and thanked. As the resident Temple cat I would observe the celebrations but not play any part in them. Because the citizens do not hold cats in high regard my role is purely that of a protector and friend. When there is sadness I share myself with the bereaved, bringing affection and tenderness to them.

My Temple is actually three temples in one. The outer walled area encloses the space and shrine that deals with creation. The middle temple square represents life, whilst the inner-most square and altar represents death. The outer walls are of human height: high enough to keep out the evil gods who would try to enter. Symbolically, death therefore finds it hard to get to the center altar. Smaller height walls surround the inner two sanctums.

Two days ago we celebrated the first day of the three-day Festival of Purity. You wouldn't believe how noisy it was. Every one, young or old joins in to walk in processions around the rice fields, between the houses and along the palm-fringed walk paths before ending up outside the Temple. The beating of drums, the hollering of voices, the sounds of bells – anything that can make a noise is used in a frenetic cacophony of sound in order to drive away any evil spirits who may have come to make their home here since the last festival. I can assure you it was no place for a cat with sensitive hearing. I escaped to the very far edge of the rice fields where the sounds were much more muffled. The noise also disturbed the snakes, the birds, the monkeys and the dogs, all of who moved to quieter areas.

Yesterday was just the opposite – a day of silence and tranquility. Having driven the evil spirits away with all of the noise, this day of silence is celebrated as a safe day; a day where thoughts are about family, the beauty of this island and how fortunate we are to dwell in safety and abundance. No work is undertaken, just meditation and the renewing of the peacefulness of the inner spirit. Thus we once more find affinity with the peaceful river of life as it flows invisibly throughout the island.

Day three is the beginning of the new season of peace and earthly abundance that we reap from cultivation of the soil. It is a feast day, a day to share with family and neighbors. The women rise early in order to prepare their food offerings. These are elaborately decorated and carried to the Temple as magnificent headpieces. After every attendee and all the food has arrived the priest blesses the gathered group, the bountiful food offerings and gives prayers for the coming season.

Wayan was on his knees at the edge of the group.

I was sitting quietly in the warm sunshine watching all this and listening to the hypnotic sound of the music group when my alert eye saw a movement just near where Wayan and the other villagers were praying.

Indeed on closer inspection, it was my dreaded enemy, King Cobra. He had been disturbed from his hiding place and was now on the move. Being behind the line of those in prayer they knew nothing of his presence.

When I saw him slithering toward my beloved Wayan I immediately sprang in to action. Along the top of the low wall and onto the lowest branch of the overhanging apple tree I moved – silently, quickly and in my crouching attack position. Nobody saw me as they were all deep in prayer and facing away from me. I moved as quickly as I could – but it was too late.

As I leapt on to the tree branch I saw the deadly brown body move forward, unveil its evil-looking hood and spit its poison into the nearest human flesh.

Wayan had been bitten on the sole of his foot.

Though I was too late to stop the attack, I leapt with all my strength on to the poisonous reptile. I knew that I was no match for the strength of the snake but at least I could delay his escape whilst the villagers found a means to entrap this intruder. I dug my claws into his upper body scales whilst biting into the softer flesh at the back of the hood. I heard Wayan cry out in pain quickly followed by the sounds of the villagers as they accessed the situation.

The cry went out for sticks and a basket for they instantly knew that the cobra must be contained. They would not kill the snake as my villagers did not believe in such killings, but they would capture it and in due course have it taken high into the mountains and released to live a life away from human habitation.

Hands quickly surrounded the cobra and me. Sticks and woven matting arrived to more easily contain the writhing body. A long forked stick penetrated through the crowd edging past my clinging body and soon held the reptile firmly in place on the ground. Quickly I let go and escaped between the flurry of legs in order to find my Wayan.

He had been placed on the ground with his foot supported on a large basket. Such bites can be fatal if not quickly attended to. Already an elder with some first aid training was attending to him. The foot had been lanced with a knife and was being squeezed, thus ejecting blood and hopefully poison if there was any there. A doctor was too far away so these local and immediate efforts had to be tried first before any thought of transporting Wayan to the distant medical help. Not all cobra bites produce poison so as the minutes ticked by and Wayan showed no signs of droopy eyes or irregular breathing there was just a chance that he had been bitten dry – that is, the cobra did not see his foot as an enemy to be killed but rather as an impediment to movement within his territory. Cobras have this ability to decide how much venom to extrude. So in due course my beloved Wayan was declared to have been bitten – but not with poison.

With the attacker safely enclosed in a large container,

Wayan's foot firmly bandaged and my bravery status confirmed by all, the ceremony and the prayers of thankfulness recommenced. Now the prayers contained an extra degree of thankfulness – for the life of Wayan being spared. The feast continued well into the night and my bowl of milk and meat portions was never empty.

Over the following days Wayan's foot recovered sufficiently for him to travel to the city and to confirm that indeed as first-born in the family, his land was secure. He and any sons from his intended marriage would as tradition demanded, inherit his land.

And so it is that my life continues peacefully, calmly and with a little more reverence from the human population than previously. Each morning as is tradition, Wayan and I take the ducks to the rice fields where they graze whilst he plants and harvests the crops and I sleep and dream in the shade of the nearby vegetation.

Of course, there's also time to be as one with the natural rhythms of the seasons and of nature. We share time to sit and ponder our thoughts, enjoy the sunshine, marvel at the insects as they fly and crawl and watch the birds as they wade and find tasty morsels. We keep an eye open for snakes of course. But most of all we take time to give thanks to the gods who created us, for we are part of them and a connected living part of all creation.

I am a very fortunate cat!

 # Old Tom

'What's up?" said the kindly voice to the sniffly kitten. "You have been crying and your eyes are all red."

"I've lost my Mama, and I'm all alone," sniffled the kitten to Old Tom.

"Well, we'll have to do something about that, won't we?" responded the kindly, but gruff old voice. "You can stay with me tonight, but tomorrow you'll have to begin your journey to find your new home."

And with that, Old Tom nosed the saucer of milk a little closer to the kitten.

As he had a want to do, Old Tom had been wandering around the disused orchard on that lazy day in late spring. The farm hadn't yet sold but the owners were being forced to move out anyway. Prices were low that year and the farmer reckoned that the city offered the best chance of employment for himself and schooling for his kids. Arnie just piled the old car as full as he could, strapped more on the roof, put his wife and two kids inside, and without so much as a last look back, headed for the unknown city beyond the horizon.

Old Tom belonged to the widow next door. She was kind

and gentle, and did the best she could with her arthritic leg and little income. Old Tom could remember the good old days when the widower's husband ran chickens, grew vegetables, caught the occasional fish and even for a time, milked a cow. Food was abundant and frequent, and Old Tom chose to live the life of a very satisfied country cat.

But times had changed. The rural economy was very depressed, with most farming families barely managing to exist. The halcyon days of abundance were over for both farmer and cat. Hence it was that Old Tom would spend his days strolling around the abandoned farm orchard, chasing the occasional mouse in the dilapidated barn and dreaming of the days when he was young enough to chase and catch any female cat he desired.

As he sat gazing at the kitten scoffing the milk, he realized that his heart was filling with grief and pain. He had recently had an unexpected opportunity to prove his ailing sexual prowess, and this kitten was a result of that union. Only that morning had he discovered the mother had been killed by a speeding milk truck, and when he went to investigate her probable birthing sites, he found the three kittens, two of which were already dead.

Life was going to be difficult for the young survivor, but his future lay in another place where he would find companionship, warmth and a reliable food supply.

The kitten was not strong, and so it was that Old Tom relented, and kept his heir with him an extra few weeks whilst the boy gained strength for the journey ahead.

For those of you, who have not had the privilege of being a father, let me say that emotionally it is something that is wholly unexpected. There is a primal feeling that is buried deep inside you that you are not aware even exists. The act of copulation, the loving feelings towards your partner during pregnancy, the miracle that is taking place inside her body. They do not prepare you for the first time you see, touch and lick your offspring. You look upon that tiny little body and wonder where it came from. How could something so tiny, so perfect, so helpless have begun its journey from a tiny seed that you have never seen? This sense of wonderment lasts but a short time, as there comes from deep within the father a great sense of pride, a feeling of "Hey, that little guy is mine. Isn't he just the best kitten in all the world." And so a new life begins in pure innocence, waiting to be molded by the events that time and the environment will inflict upon him.

Old Tom had been granted a precious few weeks with his son. No doubt it would be his last kitten, and therefore Old Tom felt that there were things that he had to tell his son. In many animal societies, as well in your human tribes, there is a tradition of verbally passing down tribal history, traditions and folklore especially to the sons.

And Old Tom did the same to me.

He spoke about many things. He imparted practical information - how to choose your permanent provider, how to wash those difficult parts of the body like under the chin and behind the ears, how to drink milk by rolling the tongue under rather than over, the potential joys of mating, and what plants will assist in healing wounds.

He talked of the importance of acting - how to attract a meal by using downcast eyes and a whimpered "meow", how to appear superior to all dogs whatever their size or barking ability, how to tell your provider of your food and comfort likes and dislikes, and how to attract and win over a suitable sexual partner should that be applicable.

And he imbued me with the proud history of our race. Of our revered life in ancient Egypt, our travels across the continents during the Renaissance, the horrors of the Dark Ages and the burnings in the name of witchcraft, all the way through to the modern acceptance of the cat as the symbol of domestic bliss. He told of interbreeding and the enormous number of different species of cat now populating across the world.

And of course, he shared with me the Secrets of the Ancients. As is tradition, I'm not at liberty to divulge these to any other cat other than to my eldest son and certainly not to any human being. Suffice to say, that we cats are here to make your journey an easier one. We are attuned to the forces of the universe, to the ebb and flow of the vibrations that you emanate, to provide sustenance to the hunger of loneliness that besets so many of you, and to provide the love and companionship that teaches you and your children the joys of respect, responsibility and reverence.

How we innately know of these things must remain a secret within the feline world. Just go about your daily business, and you will find us patiently waiting to love you as soon as you take the time to care for another beyond your own self.

As young and immature as I was, those few weeks with my father provided memories that are seared into my mind like a layer of gold. He was tender, dramatic, enthusiastic and just simply wonderful as he verbally poured forth all the highest ideals and optimism that the universe could give his son. In me, he said, he saw his future. Through me he would be young again. He would sleep contented knowing that his link in the great chain of life had moved a link further on, and would, in the passing of time, continue yet another link beyond me. A father possesses a great inner urge to make life for the next generation bigger and better and brighter than what he has achieved and experienced for himself. To give his son optimism, hope, ideals for a better world, a comfortable passage to adulthood. Instinctively he knows his own time is passing, and that the journey ahead for the youngster is purely in the paws of that youngster. Once the young mind has been set upon his journey, the body and mind of the father dissolves into a period of contentment, of "I can do no more for him now", until, inevitably, the forces of the universe recall the father's spirit from the earth-plane.

I, the youngest offspring of Old Tom, have now risen to the position of mature earth-cat, bearer of love, harbinger of truth, holder of tradition, proud bearer of the Ancient Feline Wisdoms.

I know not as yet what happened to my father.

Because of separation at kitten-hood to different families, we felines rarely know of life and death in relation to our parents or fellow siblings. We do understand that in your human society there are family and friendship bonds that last a lifetime - and it is important to your contentment in life that you have an understanding of how and where others you have met live their life. It's not just we cats who have a natural curiosity and a need to 'put to rest' unanswered questions.

But there is a different way for us to know about our friends and relatives. In us, we have an instinct, a dreaming and an ability to travel and communicate through other dimensions.

Look upon us as our eyelids quiver during sleep and you will know that we are somewhere far, far away. We are traveling the astral roads of the universe, meeting our past, observing other worlds and possibly preparing our destiny. Leave us continue to sleep at these times, for perhaps on that day, we too, have an appointment with a spirit beyond the grave.

During these dreamtimes we receive answers to our questions. If we have questions of a spiritual nature then the Ancients visit us and take our spirit to places and to teachers where we will learn and understand.

If it is unknown to us that loved ones have died, then we can meet up with their spirit and once more share the connection of family and bonding.

If our loved ones are still alive we can be transported in our dreams to where they live. Like a spirit we can just observe them without communication or we can send vibrations to them and communicate our love and our presence to them. You've no doubt observed the whiskers of your cat twitching during his sleep. As well as this meaning a happy dream for him, it can also indicate that a communication is underway between loved ones.

And have you been quietly sitting with or near your cat and out the corner of your eye you sense that you saw movement? If your cat stirs as if hearing a strange sound then you most certainly have observed a feline loved one having a spiritual visit. And isn't it delightful to understand that even though hearts may be beating many hundreds of miles apart, that communication on a vibration and ethereal level can still take place. Just look at human twins and how they can silently communicate across vast distances.

Therefore when I re-meet my father in this spiritual way, I will lick his face, and purr contentedly knowing that my heart is filled with love.

And I will say "Thank you father, for sharing your most precious gifts with me - your time, your heritage and your loving heart."

104

 **Wee Folk**

Humans are such disbelievers! Your entire world seemingly has to be looked at from human height. And if you can't see it, then you won't believe in it!

Consequently there are only a very few of you who are chosen to be privileged to enter the other worlds that co-exist with yours. So, to be one of the privileged, open your mind and let me tell you my tale...

Leprechauns. Fairies. Elves. Mermaids. Sea Sprites. They and many other so-called myths *do* exist. My involvement with the little people who live at the bottom of the garden began when my mistress and I rented a lovely old mansion for a short late summer vacation.

After driving for several hours along ever narrowing roads we came to the fork in the road we were looking for. And, as was scribbled on the note my mistress constantly referred to, on our left was the overgrown entrance to "Bramble Manor". The mailbox had not seen a letter in a very long time. The aptly named brambles had begun to entwine the gateposts and the cast-iron gate creaked with an agonizing groan as my mistress slowly pushed it open.

It was late afternoon as the car meandered along the overgrown driveway towards the two-storey stone house. As I peered out through the car windows I could see that the garden had been neglected for a very long time. How wonderful it was going to be to spend my days exploring that heavily vegetated utopia. Instinctively I knew that I was going to like it there.

That evening we were both exhausted from our journey and we retired early. I found a padded window ledge at the top of the stairs that allowed me to look out into the garden, but sleep very quickly took hold and the view had to wait until the next day.

The old grandfather clock had just chimed two when I opened my sleepy eyes to see a family of mice scurrying across the landing and in behind the surrounds of the open fireplace. The moonlight filled the room and I observed that the only creature asleep in the house that night was my mistress.

Out in the garden I could sense a great deal more movement. And right at the back of the garden, near where it joined the nearby forest, there was an area of light. A phosphorescent glow permeated the dark vegetation and it was near this area that much of the movement was taking place. But whatever it was, I presumed that it would still be there tomorrow.

Making a mental note of the location I drifted back to sleep, not waking until the golden rays of the morning sun began to warm my coat.

After a plate of my favorite food and a saucer of full cream country milk, I was ready to explore my new domain. The garden was really quite vast, spreading from the house herb garden, down the gentle slopes past the vegetables, more flowerbeds and the orchard, before merging into the edge of the forest. Whoever had designed the garden knew that one of the secrets to making it interesting was to have a myriad of twists and turns so that the explorer would have constant new delights as they moved in any direction. And so it was with me.

Firstly there were the mixed aromas of the herb garden. As I brushed past each plant, frequently breaking a leaf or two, each plant gave off their aromatic specialty. The delightful pineapple mint particularly appealed to me, and it's mild tropical aroma stayed in my fur for many hours.

Nearby was the vegetable garden, now grossly overrun with weeds and leaf-eating insects. What vegetables were there had been self-sown resulting in carrot shouldering pumpkin, pea entwining the corn, and lettuce and cabbage growing leafy hearts like warrior kings. It appeared that no one had harvested any of the gardens for a very long time so it had become the survival of the fittest.

It was a wonderful site to explore at my height, akin to what I imagine it would be like for you to get through a tropical jungle. There were huge pumpkin leaves to hide under, massed forests of carrot tops that tickled and tantalized the fur as you sidled through them. Entangled canopies of pea vines let down their tendrils to ensnare the unsuspecting intruder. And tall forests of celery, corn and broad bean reached skyward like green guardians barring the entrance to a forbidden land. This was indeed wonderful territory for adventure, and to find the unexpected.

Next to the vegetables was an amazing tangle of overgrown shrubbery that upon reflection still bore a resemblance to an earlier life as a maze. Now, I didn't know it was a maze until I tried to edge my way towards the forest that I could just see above the tops of the shrubbery. Retracing my steps by way of my scent proved somewhat more difficult than I had expected particularly as my nostrils were heavy with a mixture of various herbs, including the afore-mentioned pineapple mint.

But, it was a glorious end-of-summer morning and time wasn't a pressing need. After many false starts, blocked pathways and a startled bird or two, I did what any self-respecting cat would do. I jumped up onto an appropriate branch, climbed to the top and in my mind plotted my way to the exit nearest the forest.

This proved to be easier said than done. After an exasperating dead-end was reached, the only solution was to go under the foliage. When I saw an appropriate break in the undergrowth I crouched onto all fours and slowly dragged myself through the miniature pine needles and out into a flower garden - a flower garden so beautiful that my whole body tingled with the sight of such a profusion of color.

As I looked up from my crouched, ground level position, I could see all around me the delights of a cottage garden in full bloom, a profusion of self-seeded color and entanglement. Hollyhocks, snapdragons, marigolds, irises, pansies as well as exquisite roses of seemingly every color and size. There must have been dozens of species, and hundreds and hundreds of plants. The air was filled with the most exquisite fragrant aromas. The low drone of the bees at work could be heard above the rustle of the dancing foliage. Butterflies, so brilliantly patterned that you imagined they had just escaped from an artist's palette, mingled in flight with the delicate translucent seedpods that were being wafted on the breeze to germinate in distant parts of the garden.

Throughout my meanderings in the maze I had become distinctly uncomfortable. It was as if I was being watched, a feeling that I was not alone, yet I could see no other life except the occasional bird and the constant dive-bombing of the dragonflies.

And here in this touch of heaven, I felt the presence even more strongly. As I looked around the garden beds, my eyes alighted on the nearby fernery, and in particular, the circle of white stones beneath the largest of the fronds.

It was only then I realized that without knowing it, and quite by accident, I had discovered a fairy garden. What a klutz I had been not to recognize the signs. The birds had been watching me and sending out messages about my progress, the dragonflies were dive-bombing me to distract my attention and the fairy lookouts and their butterfly assistants had been all around me, well hidden by the tangled foliage.

And there, sitting on the centre stone, was a fairy. Even the reflected golden haze of the morning sun could not detract from her exquisite beauty. Her body was as fine and smooth as the most delicate silk, with her wings as translucent as the sheerest gossamer spray. And her aura glowed as if airbrushed in phosphorous by the most adept of artists. If this was a dream, it was a dream that I would have gladly traded several lives to be part of. Oh dear reader, you can only imagine how rare such a discovery can be, a moment that so few are privileged to partake of. Yet I could see that it was all real.

And when the fairy realized that I had seen her, she vaporized in a cloud of pixie dust. As I looked around the garden, now much more intently than previously, I began to discern other movement. Other wee folk were there sitting on the shrubbery branches, counting petals on the daisy flowers and lazily kicking seeds along the garden floor. And if I might say so, they all looked decidedly mournful, not at all the image of a happy kingdom as enshrined in children's picture books.

I was bold enough to purr this observation to a little gnome who I spied sitting on a nearby toadstool. He was exactly how you would imagine him to look - red hat, green clothing, white beard, and boots with laces. But so sad!

He responded with a sniffle, "They've taken the Princess and are holding her to ransom. Their magic is stronger than ours and we don't know what to do."

As a cat I was generally regarded as an unwelcome intruder into their world, but even with the burden of all their problems, the little people treated me as a friend. Soon I was surrounded by a mass of wee folk - fairies, gnomes, sprites, pixies, butterflies and more - all eager to share their despair and anguish with me.

It seemed that the Fairy Princess had been kidnapped by a tribe of hobgoblins who lived and scavenged near the edge of the nearby forest. They were creatures of the night that sought to enslave the wee folk to look after their every need. Because of the human desecration of the forests there was now only a handful of them remaining, but enough to make life miserable for my new friends. The tribe members lived by their wits, meddled with a rather inept knowledge of magic and made occasional forays into the garden in search of more slaves and additional magic.

And so it was on one of these occasions that the Fairy Princess was captured.

"How will you rescue her?" I enquired. But nobody seemed to know. They just continued to sob for their kidnapped friend.

"Perhaps you could help us," said the gnome. "You're bigger

than we are. Perhaps you could scare them."

"Or eat them," chimed in another pixie voice.

"Or lead us into battle," retorted a deep voice from the depths of the agapanthus.

It transpired that this latter voice belonged to Purcell, a somewhat roguish pixie, whose looks mirrored a lifetime of adventure and misadventure.

"I say that we organize a rescue mission. And you, cat, will lead us."

What are they saying? I'd just come up here with my mistress for a quiet few days in the country, and here I am being conscripted to lead a search party to rescue a Fairy Princess. My cat friends back in the city just wouldn't believe it, would *not* believe it!

But as with all of life, universal forces place you in just the right place at just the right time. And being an adventurous cat, how could I refuse to help friends in trouble?

As the noonday sun shone warmly on that garden patch, a plot of magic and merry-do was being hatched. A plot that would have the Princess rescued and returned before the full moon of the Fall Equinox could cast its first magical moonbeam.

All that afternoon the wee folk worked at a frantic pace. Some were seen to be sewing; others were gathering piles of acorns and other seedpods. Others were seen to be flying, buzzing or scurrying in all directions intent on succeeding in the task that they had been allotted.

Whilst all this feverish activity was taking place, I went on a reconnaissance mission. After all, who would take any notice of a roving cat that just happened to be intent on exploring this long-forgotten corner of the world? Even so, I took my role seriously, as it was I who had to lead the expedition. My memory of the terrain, the obstacles, the open areas, and the potential traps were therefore of primary importance to its success.

Around past the algae-covered swimming pool, through the still blossoming orchard, past the lavender hedge, over the low stone fence and into the forest I went.

However, the warmth of that last summer's day did not follow me beyond the wall. No, there instead, was the damp, dark gloom of evil. The carpet of long dead forest leaves gave you a shiver when your paw walked on them. The shadow of the trees purveyed an evil enchantment that seemed to personify the hobgoblin dance of deceit and mistrust. The wind continuously whined and groaned an agonized path through the trees.

This was no place for man or beast. This was a place of nightmares.

Cautiously I moved amongst the trees, bounded across the open areas and slipped quietly from tree branch to tree branch wherever I could. Finally, the smoke rising from the campfire told me that my goal was in sight. As I peered down from my treetop vantage point I could see what appeared to be a birdcage hanging from a branch. It was causing great amusement to the assembled hobgoblins. A warm, golden glow surrounded this prison, a glow like a lighthouse beacon in a turbulent sea. I knew now that this was where they were keeping the Princess.

That night, my new friends and I would return to rescue her. But now I had to report my findings to the others.

As the mauve-edged clouds swelled in the evening sky, we held one final meeting in the dell. The Queen, sitting above us all on an old brass tap handle, directed the briefing. Sitting in a fairy circle were her subjects, led by the cunning old Purcell. After I had reported back my observations, he checked and double-checked everyone's battle plan.

It was to go like this. Purcell and I would lead the expedition. He would be a jockey upon my neck, his legs buried in my fur, his hands holding onto my collar. He could then be carried right into the middle of the hobgoblin camp. Whilst I distracted the enemy, he would be joined by a band of other pixies who would silently be delivered into the camp on the backs of butterflies and moths.

Waiting at the stone fence on the edge of the forest would be the dragonfly army. When the appropriate signal was given, they would attack the hobgoblins en-masse and be joined by two swarms of worker bees. Should any pursuing hobgoblins reach the garden area, the fairies, the spiders, the mice, the fruit bats and all manner of other wee folk hidden in the foliage were prepared to entangle, trip, bite, spray, and otherwise hinder the common enemy.

On my back and attached to my collar, there had been prepared a small leather harness, big enough to hold Purcell and the Princess. As I was to lead the escape back to the garden it was imperative that I remained highly maneuverable even whilst carrying my valuable cargo.

As Purcell and I jumped down from the stone fence into the creeping evil of the forest, the moon made its first appearance. Its silvery-grey light gave us a better view than we would have otherwise had, but it also etched the tree branches with light, giving them the appearance of gnarled and ghostly armies of the night. The wind continued to moan its rasping malevolence, giving my skin a delectable mix of adrenalin-induced excitement with a fear of black magic and villainy. My tail fairly bristled with anticipation.

Ahead was the light of the enemy camp, my nostrils insistent that the air there was pungent with evil and witchery. Crouched in the grass we watched their bawdy merriment. Purcell leaned forward whispering instructions in my ear. Slowly we stalked our way through the darkness created by the forest canopy until we reached the tree from which the Princess and her cage were suspended.

We noticed several lookouts, but they were all engrossed with the fireside activities. In a single bound I was up the trunk of the tree and onto a heavily foliaged branch. Purcell wished me well as he slid from my back and on to the branch. His job was to open the cage and rescue the Princess whilst I diverted attention from the tree. Above us there was a rustle of leaves as the moths and butterflies alighted the additional pixie troops.

As I sat high in the tree, looking down on the dancing and feasting, I chose my mark. There, to the left of the fire, surrounded by a small group of his cohorts, sat the leader of this rabble. A leap into the middle of this band would definitely cause the chaos we required. With a wink and a blink, I jumped.

Gazooks! What chaos my leap caused! I haven't seen such pandemonium since I chased a mouse through the ladies lingerie department. So much shouting and running and confusion!

Whilst this was all happening, Purcell and his group were hopefully rescuing the Princess. We knew we only had a few short minutes to maintain the diversion, so when I saw a sprinkling of fairy dust waft down from the cage I knew it was time to make my escape.

Deftly evading my would-be captors, I moved quickly to the base of the tree where I sprang to the first bough and headed for the cage. There I saw the phosphoric glow of the Princess. Purcell and his army had done well.

"On to my back. Quickly. Quickly," I demanded.

But by now the base of the tree had been surrounded by the meanest and angriest group of hobgoblins that you would ever hope not to find. Escape was not going to be easy.

Fortunately, as arranged, my leap had signaled the aerial forces. In a short time the massed drone of the bees could be heard above the agitated voices. And then the dive-bombing squadron of dragonflies began their sorties.

Above us, the commando pixies were clambering aboard their aerial chariots. And as the carrier of the commander and the Princess, all that was needed of me was to find a way through all this. I sat crouched on the bough waiting for my moment.

"Hold on you two. This is going to be one exciting chase," I meowed.

With the fairy-dust glow of the Princess shining on my head like a beacon, I was the obvious centre of attention and had to be stopped. With the inherited instinct of a thousand generations, I patiently awaited my opportunity. It came, and like a cheetah with its eyes fixed on its quarry, I leapt beyond the immediate mayhem, and headed for the stone fence.

Through the darkness I raced, passing under the cloud of droning bees, on across the clammy leaf-covered forest floor and into the moonlit clearing. Ahead were the stone-fence and the safety of the garden on the other side. Behind me I could hear the tumult of battle, the anger of voices that had been wronged. Of yelps and shouts as stings made their marks. Of low droning like a school of sleeping children. Of wings fluttering in the night air carrying homeward their exhausted troops.

On my head I could feel the jubilance of my two jockeys as they sat upright in their holsters, their clench fists raised in defiance to our pursuers, their legs gripped around my neck, encouraging me to even greater speed.

Across the fence we leapt and into the safety of the garden. Immediately friends surrounded us, and it was there that the last of the hobgoblin rabble would have to be routed. Three of them had continued to pursue me and now they were climbing the fence. The glow of light from the Princess again acted like a beacon, so they knew my position. When they came down from the fence, they came straight towards me.

To re-enter *our* world was their big mistake. The garden troops were ready, hidden like silent specters melting into the moonlit shadows. This moment had been imagined and then meticulously choreographed by Purcell and it was up to him to give them the signal. The light from the Princess allowed him to be seen by his troops, so like a silhouetted orchestral conductor, he directed the battle.

Slingshots filled with seeds and pinecones were released. Spider-web tripwires crisscrossed the pathway, fruit bats dive-bombed with rotting vegetables, mice skirted between unwary legs, and fairy and pixie dust mingled with pollen and formed a sticky air-borne cloud.

Overhead, a re-grouped aerial armada of dragonflies, with

pixie jockeys aboard, carried ground-pepper bomb-bags that soon had all participants in the affray sneezing and rubbing their eyes. After one particularly heavy bombing run, I sneezed so frightfully loudly that my passengers were sent sprawling across the lavender and into the parsnips.

But if I do say so myself, it was the sneeze that won the war!

Can you imagine that moonlit sight of me, exploding like a bomb? A huge bundle of disheveled fluff accompanied by a sneeze-blast that released a fur-ball of significant proportions right into the midst of the hobgoblin attack.

That was all too much for the enemy. They indicated to each other that retreat was the only solution.

And so to the cheers and merriment of the guardians of the garden, they were last seen yelping and cursing as they scrambled across the wall heading back to the forest, never to be seen again.

The Princess had been successfully rescued and could once more take her rightful place in the fairyland hierarchy.

As the village church bell chimed midnight, the Equinox celebrations were in full swing in the lower garden. As resident hero, I was feted with all kinds of fairy food, pixie gymnastic demonstrations, butterfly dancing and dandelion wine. The night was filled with a happiness and celebration that only comes from hearts that are free from fear and uncertainty. The Princess looked radiant.

If you had looked out the house window that night you would have been aware of a glow in the garden. A patch of St Elmo's fire you could have thought, a trick of the moonlight, marsh fog - or just your intoxicated mind playing games with you. It wouldn't matter.

But, there in that isolated garden that night, a life and death drama had been fought and won. A little patch of peace had been planted on this earth and like the garden itself, the peace would grow and multiply if tended, nourished and cared for.

That night we partied until sunrise - the fairies, the beetles, the pixies, the sprites, the butterflies, the mice, the bats, the worms, the spiders and I. All of us different and diverse creatures of this earth, yet we had battled as one against a common foe, and it was peace who was the victor.

During the morning I slept the sleep of the contented heart. I dreamed of the things that are, and the things that could be, and the things that should be.

I dreamed a hope that my nine lives would remain as peaceful as that country morning on the first glorious day of fall.

And for you, my good friend, my story time listener and companion, my wish is that your heart will also continue to be filled with the peace, contentment and happiness that comes from loving your cat.

Cuddle us frequently and you will be richly rewarded. Share

your hopes and fears and dreams with us, and we will guide you and protect you. Pat us and we will banish your loneliness. Feed us and we will fill your soul with an abundance of love. We care not for your clothes, your money or your possessions. Our love is unconditional. Cuddle us and love us as your perfect soul mate.

Then, together, we can share the dreams of the angels and live in a world of peace and contentment and neighborly love just as the fairies now do at the bottom of that wonderful garden.

Accident

I love sitting high up in the elm looking down on my world. From here I can see as much of the world as I want to see. I know from the television and what the postman brings that there is an amazing world beyond the horizon that I can see from my tree, but I'm happy here in my patch. I'm not seeking high adventure in strange locales, or meeting other cats who live in the city, or wanting to travel the high seas on cruise liners. I don't need to place myself in awkward or testing situations. I don't have that overt curiosity that according to human urban myth will lead to my death nine times over – all I require here is my master's milk, food and the warm appreciative comfort of companionship.

There he is now – sitting in his motorized wheelchair soaking up the warm, mid-morning sunshine. Since the accident he's not been the man who shared my kitten-hood with me. In those days he would wake early, whistle as he showered, feed me my morning meat as he made and ate his toast, and with a frolicsome cuddle, a gentle rub on my head and a long firm stroke of energy along my back, he would depart for "the office". The rest of the day was mine to enjoy until I heard that car engine sound coming up the driveway. As my mother taught me, like a dutiful cat I would always be at the door in time for his arrival and of course, share a close rub of my body against his trouser leg. This was my welcome home for him. Together we have been the best of companions.

Evenings were spent together on the couch watching television, or I sat purring on his outstretched leg as he read. How nice it was whenever his hand idly massaged my fur or when he let me snooze on his chest and I could feel his heartbeat synchronizing with mine.

He was a solitary man so we had few visitors though he talked on the telephone and communicated via the internet with friends and colleagues all over the world. I did so enjoy sitting on the warm modem box near his computer. From there I could see images of the outside world, see people talking to him from their homes somewhere way beyond the horizon, and watch him write his emails.

I could understand some of what he wrote as I had a good command of English. Perhaps you don't realize this, but just as babies hear language spoken all around them and they absorb the words until they can verbalize them, so it is with cats. Certainly we can't (or don't want to) speak "human", but we can certainly understand in our head exactly what is being talked or written about. We will never understand everything, but we know enough to understand much more than you think we do. When it suits us, we simply ignore your directions or questions and pretend that we don't understand. But really it's our choice, so we keep the status quo by acting and being quintessentially feline whilst fully understanding the reality of what is going on.

This is a special trait that cats have. All around us human life can be happening - the storms of emotions raging, the minutiae of human existence unfolding, the desires for betterment being pursued - yet we are happy just being ourselves. We conserve our energies, we have inner peace and calmness, we absorb simple happiness from the natural world around us, and we are not trying to be the biggest, the best or the richest. We simply exist and we are happy. We make our own happiness and contentment, and that puts us at one with the life forces. We are not fighting against the energy stream nor are we fighting others. Life is a pleasure.

But for a human who loses the use of part of his body, the pleasure of living can seem a thing of the past. And so it is with my master. His legs no longer function well enough for him to stand on them unaided. He needs assistance to bathe, to visit the bathroom, to undress. His caregiver visits twice a day to assist, and Mrs. Arbuthnot comes for a few hours every couple of days to do a little cleaning and to cook meals that he can heat in the microwave. So he is well looked after.

But it was his spirit for living – or the lack thereof – that concerned me. Before the accident he had a focus on his work in the city, he enjoyed his garden and tinkering with the house to make it just the way he wanted it, he laughed and whistled and had a smile for his neighbors. He liked

125

reading, communicating with his distantly located friends and colleagues, and his music, especially playing his guitar.

After his return from hospital, his mind was in a different place from what I had previously observed. There was emptiness about his eyes, his energy seemed to have departed his body and his interest in his surroundings was non-existent. I did my bit to rekindle his spirit. I jumped and rolled and did all those things that make one look a bit foolish, but will bring a smile back to a jaded face. I did manage to observe a smile or three but it didn't last long. But we did have wonderful hours together as I sat on his knee in the wheelchair. Together we both dozed in the warm sunshine and felt the deep bond of two friends harmoniously sharing time together.

Instinctively I knew he needed more than I could give. He needed a purpose in life, someone to inspire and reactivate his spirit, someone to literally lend him a hand to get back to living. I'd heard the doctor say that walking was certainly still possible, but it wouldn't happen without effort on his part. The longer he delayed his rehabilitation the harder the journey would be and the less likelihood of success.

What a dark time it is in one's life when the life force that normally energizes us reduces to a mere trickle and we only continue to exist by default.

But no matter how dark the night or how low the spirit there is the unseen hand of the universe at work. Whether we know it or not, we all have angels and guardians and healing spirits with us on our earth journey. As part of our decision to be born into humanity and to live an earthly existence we are given a support team and we are not expected to journey without them. Many humans of this world don't know of or would care about such invisible support. They live their lives in a hedonistic, ego-driven, individualist way.

But to others who are sensitive to such knowledge, they cannot imagine a moment without the support of their team. Whilst not a spiritual or religious man, my master knew that miracles can happen. He often wondered why the traveling salesman happened to be at his mother's isolated farmhouse at the precise moment she had her heart attack. And why a total stranger saved his brother Kevin from an upturned dinghy when the boy couldn't swim. He was not averse to the idea that we are helped from the other side in times of danger, especially if we still have work to do here on the earth-plane before we die.

I am a great believer in spirit helpers. But during those weeks that my master sat in that wheelchair hardly moving or observing, even I began to wonder about the time that the other side was taking to get my master living again. I appreciate that their time-frame has nothing to do with ours, and we are always impatient for action whilst they see that they have all of eternity to act. But being a cat, my patience won out and I instinctively knew that sooner or later – and probably from the most unexpected source – the key to his reactivation would come. All we had to do was wait.

And so, in the fullness of time, it did come. In the guise of his long lost brother, Kevin.

Many years ago, the various siblings left the farm to find their own route to happiness. Some went to the city, some overseas. The bonds of family were not strongly in evidence so it was a great surprise to my master to receive the email to say that Kevin was coming to stay. Naturally he told Kevin that he was unable to look after him, that it was a bad time to come. But Kevin duly arrived on the appointed day.

My first impressions of him proved correct.

We felines can see dimensions that most humans cannot. One of these is to be able to read an aura, that remarkable colored energy field that surrounds all living things. Depending on the energy and vitality of the subject, so it radiates around them. To the uninitiated you could describe it as a rainbow glow, with different colors stronger or weaker depending on the health of that part of the body. One can instantly see which parts are healthy and which ones are not.

As Kevin walked up the path and was welcomed into the house, I could see that the colors of his stomach indicated a serious health issue. His joviality, his good humor and the sheer joy of his seeing his brother again hid any indication that all was not well in his body.

Over the next few days Kevin settled into the household and began to get it much more organized and functioning more efficiently. He took on some of the caregiver duties, helped Mrs. Arbuthnot cook food and he, being the handyman that he was, began to repair aspects of the house needing attention and to spend some time in the garden. He was filled with energy and a new purpose in helping his brother.

About a week in I could see a change was taking place in my master's demeanor. There was an eagerness for conversation to catch up on all the lost years of news of family members. There was an increasing appetite for food, of sharing a bottle of wine, of asking questions about the world. It was like a reawakening was beginning to happen and a new sibling affinity was being linked. It was not without its moments of "why me" and "I'm no longer useful to myself or the world" conversations but these were becoming fewer in number.

It was during one of those wine-assisted dinners that the moment happened.

I was drifting in and out of sleep on the third shelf of the bookcase when Kevin admitted that he had stomach cancer. For a moment it was as if all the air had been sucked out of the room – like that totally still period on a summer's day just before a storm arrives. My master gave of a large silent expletive and sat there in his wheelchair aghast at this unexpected news. "I've known for a while now, and the doctors think that it is probably inoperable and therefore terminal. That's why I've come back – for more tests."

To my master this was an epiphany moment - a fraction of a

second that changed the balance of his mind from inward looking to outward looking, from self-pity to love for another, from "why me" to "I must help him".

When one takes the emphasis off one's own dilemmas and concentrates on helping others then there is a joyous reuniting with the stream of life. Loving one another is the universal bond that is surely the kernel of our earthly existence.

That night I listened intently as plans were formulated to financially assist Kevin to have all the tests he could possibly have, that he was welcome to live at the house as long as he liked and that together they would find a solution to the condition.

Over the following days you could feel the frustrations of a wheelchair-bound spirit. My master became impatient to free himself from those shackles. There was a new determination in his spirit to exercise his legs back to being strong enough to support his body, and then, to walk again, free of any support. In due course all of this would happen.

Periodically Kevin would leave us for extended periods in the city hospitals returning for recuperation and renewal of both his body and spirit.

On his return I would spend happy hours beside him on his bed or accompany him for short walks in the garden. As my master regained his strength, my time on his lap became less common, less required. As both of them struggled with their demons, I became an important diversion for them.

They played with me, cared for me, spent time with me, slept beside me and in all ways made me the happiest cat. Each saw themselves as the caregivers for the other, but like all caregivers they also needed other interests to balance that intensity. And much to my constant delight, I was the one they focused on.

What have I learned from my life with these two men? Never give up hope, that family can be a great source of love, that the eternal inner spirit lives on even when the human body is frail and through positive thinking it can overcome incredible odds. Yes, all of these. But also, that love for others defines us.

Karma In The Garden

Both the vegetable and the flowering garden fill my nostrils with delight. It is high summer and the fruits and the vegetables are plump with goodness having absorbed the golden vitality from the sun. And the flowers are a myriad of petals and stamens and leaves. Even the grasses are abundant and a tangle to walk through.

As I walk the paths and byways of my mistress' garden, my fur is brushed by a variety of foliage. The plants have all grown magnificently with the warmth and they certainly don't hesitate to cover a pathway or obstruct a shortcut for we felines.

It's a very different world down here from what you humans see when you gaze upon a garden. It's true what they say about it being a bit of a jungle. Down here is where it all happens.

Firstly there is the noise. You might consider a garden such a peaceful enclave but believe me it's far from that. With my sensitive hearing (and I say this on behalf of that other lot – the four-legged canine as well) it gets very noisy near ground-level. Imagine if you can, the cacophony that results from the droning of the dragonfly, the buzzing of the bees, the chomping of the caterpillar, the incessant marching of the ants, the drip, drip, drip inside the milk-thistle and the straining sounds of expanding branches. It's all enough to make one want to withdraw to the comforts of one's favorite cushion on the sunny drawing-room window.

Every plant and creature seems to be in a hurry, making merry whilst the sun still shines. Of course, if I'm having a lazy day or I'm hiding under a large bushy leaf like in the rhubarb patch, there are the visits by the birds. Chirping and fluttering and scratching the soil – and that horrible satisfied gurgling sound as their prey wriggles or is otherwise heartily consumed. The occasional small lizard races along the path, back legs pounding the earth whilst trying to stay upright whilst dancing on hot coals. Nature has left them hard-wired to a frenetic disco-dancing lifestyle. Well, I suppose someone down the food chain was in line for the wiring, so why not that it was they? You won't ever find a cat with such an unsophisticated look as that.

We who meander these vegetated pathways must always be aware, especially later in the day, of what you humans call the automated watering system! I can tell you, that a puss does not like to be so rudely awakened from her slumber or from her late afternoon constitutional that she has to leap into the air like an un-coordinated child on a trampoline. It is particularly embarrassing when such an unfortunate event is witnessed by and is the source of great amusement to others. Those children who deliberately turn on the sprinkler system and derive much amusement from my misfortune instantly become my enemy. The return karma rendered by a cat to its transgressors should not be under-estimated as was the case this last summer past.

My mistress' two grandchildren, in human years, around ten and twelve, came to stay at the mansion for a week or two of their summer holidays. They were introduced to me on their first day when I returned to the kitchen for my evening meal. The girl, the younger of the two, appeared gentle and kind, and seemed satisfied to enjoy my purring resulting from her gentle patting. The young gentleman and I did not have the same reaction to one another. It was instantly 'claws-at-one-o'clock'. As you can imagine I am not averse to adding the odd hiss or two for theatrical effect when the situation calls for it but he was trouble with a capital T!

The first day or two went by without any incident or indeed, having to see much of the children at all. They were taken to the beach, shopping and to something called an amusement arcade. My mistress seemed very happy spending time with them, but on the third day she was called away for a few hours and the children were left to roam the large house and the extensive garden as they wished. Having grown tired of the swing, pushing each other around in the wheelbarrow and chasing butterflies through the garden, it was probably inevitable that when they saw me, I was seen as a new and lively plaything.

The boy was so much quicker getting to the tap than I gave him credit for. The hose was soon gushing water and like a clown with his backside on fire, the boy, hose, water and horrendous shrieks of mirth, headed down the path, across the vegetable patch and straight to where I was waking from my afternoon slumbers. The girl was animatedly running behind him extolling him not to hurt me or to do anything stupid. Not do anything stupid!!!! Couldn't she see what was going to happen? I was the bulls-eye target for that water cannon and that monster of a boy was not going to take one iota of notice of his younger sibling.

KERSPLASHHHHHHH!!!!!! It hit me like the force of a thousand running bulls. Cold, with great force and with such a surprise that it literally catapulted me into the hot afternoon sunshine. As my four legs splayed out in very un-feline-like directions, I let out a monstrous cry of anguish and surprise, that no doubt, could be heard a considerable distance away. And then it all went quiet and I had an epiphany moment, just like when you humans are in a car accident and that split second turns into a slow-motion montage of your life and surroundings. And so it was with me.

From my height in mid-air I could see the whole garden, the girl shouting angrily at her brother, the hose twisting and turning out of control like a startled snake, the startled birds taking flight and the water droplets cascading earthward from my sleek coat. It was surreal. A moment that, in reflection, captured an instant in time, stretched it, burned it deep into my thoughts and gave me such clarity like I'd never known before – or since. I was not hurt, or in danger, or angry – I simply was at one with the universe in a single moment of time. I would have looked awkward and startled to anyone observing the scene, but inwardly I was peaceful, gliding smoothly through the warm, aroma-filled summer afternoon heat. My mind was acting clearly as I distinctly remember moving my paws in a downward direction so that my earth landing would be with four paws and not my body. After what seemed like an interminable time I touched the ground. Instantly my time-frame went back to human time. Barely had I touched the soil before I was away across the vegetables and heading for the safety of the house.

Without being observed, I immediately made straight to my favorite hiding place above the curtains in the attic. There I was safe as that room was off-limits to everyone except the mistress.

As I dried it was there that I silently and deliberately plotted my revenge. But I was thankful too. For in that moment of bullying, I flew like an angel. I was uplifted to a higher and different dimension, to a place I'd not been before. We felines have nine lives, that is true – but did you know we also have nine feline angels to look after us? That is, nine wonderful gods and goddesses from the ancient cities of the Nile and other extraordinary civilizations where cats were venerated and worshipped. They care for us, guide us, journey with us and illuminate us with divine understanding. Through us, the living animal, they bring love, serenity and insight to this earth. We are the carriers of this love and we do our best to bring this love to all we come in contact with.

And so it was as I sat on my beloved curtain pelmet in the highest place in the house, that I was reminded that as a cat

I have a duty, sworn on the sacred scrolls of the Old Empire, to be loving to all I come in contact with. Like the bullied child, eventually there is a time when you know your own path, you believe in your own self-worth and you tell your aggressor that you love them. Quite simply, love conquers the anger and quells the fire. It can be uneasy at first, the anger may again flare-up, but a seed of peace has been sown. I know enough about gardens to know that when a seed is nurtured it can mature and ripen to bring benefits to those around it.

My young man of much anger that I now hear being berated downstairs by my mistress for teasing and bullying me, has been presented to me as an example of my continual need to learn – and to put that learning into practice.

I was given a gift today – the magic of transcending earthly time – and I must repay the instigator of this magic. The boy has anger, aggression, fear, perhaps loneliness within him that outwardly displays itself in a non-loving way. Perhaps through my example of loving him irrespective of the incident, then he will, in a subtle way, know and understand that forgiveness allows us all to live together in better harmony.

Now that I am licked clean and my coat is once more shining, I shall descend the stairs, find the boy, rub myself against his leg and allow him to gently play with me.

Tonight I shall sleep contented.

 # Egyptian Gods

Museums can be wonderful places to visit. Some of course are filled with glass cases containing a bewildering array of stuffed animals (often including a heavy bias towards my near and dear). Others are all high-tech, "interactive modules spanning the epoch of human endeavor" that invite the curious visitor to partake of the knowledge on display.

Mostly the buildings are vast in size. Built when man had a need to express his perceived important place in the universe, they are monuments to grandeur. This vastness coincided with an abundance of money, new building methods and a need for whatever he built, to last forever (or at least a century or more). Mausoleums could be another word you could use for such structures. And so I would describe our local museum as such.

Walking up to the entrance is like taking a trip back to ancient Greece. Manicured lawns and cypress trees precede the vast stone steps that lead visitors up towards the giant Corinthian columns with their fluted sides and ornate capitals. Like when visiting a vast cathedral, the impression the builders have left is to dwarf the initiate at the door, overwhelm their senses and then, as they move about the building, remold their historical preconceptions.

Why such intellectual thoughts beset me as I scampered up the steps and under the giant portico I cannot imagine. I was simply here to have another look at the ancient Egyptian section and perhaps, if time permitted, a look at some of my favorite 'catafacts' (my term for artifacts that are in some way important to we cats).

The attendants were busy with the usual crowds of families and tourist groups, so it was easy to slip past them and on down the corridors. Occasionally I had to show caution and momentarily hide behind a stuffed mammal or a "Press Here To Play" gizmo in a glass case. I knew my way around fairly well, so it wasn't long before I was in the Egyptian section.

Ancient Egypt was a wonderful period of history for my feline ancestors. As the hieroglyphs illustrated, felines were revered as gods and treated accordingly. They were, of course, much slimmer in body size than some of us today, and with much less fur. After all, it was a very hot climate with no means of being cooled other than to sit on the shaded sandstone or marble, or if the gods were propitious that day, a slave boy and his feather fan would waft gentle breezes around you.

Food was a diet of whatever swam in the Nile and was caught that day, or what feathered bird ran around on two legs. Tasty fish tit-bits, occasionally some crocodile steak, some spatchcock or chicken bones, hippopotamus steak and of course, fresh milk, both cow and goat.

How do I know all this you ask? Cats have an ability to be able to time travel and I use this ability whenever I want to escape the everyday realities of this modern world. Sometimes it's just like a brief vacation but it is a particularly important ability when one is ill or suffering from injury. At those times it allows for healing from the Ancients to take place.

In the human world of today there are spiritual enlightened souls in all communities who have the ability to see into other dimensions. They can see colored auras around a person and from those colors understand what is ailing that person. Many humans dream in their sleep and this is often called astral traveling. You are still connected to your human body by way of an umbilical silver cord so that if you are disturbed, say by a sudden noise, you are back in your mortal body in a flash. This is nothing more than moving the mind to another dimension and traveling to other realms, dimensions and times. You must remember that time and calendars are human inventions so the universe has no concept of them.

Therefore when you sleep you can be in another dimension but it is only when you recall the dream in the morning that your mind connects it to an historic era. That then allows you to tell others by placing it in a time period.

So when I sleep I too, can travel to other worlds and historical times. I always enjoy a visit to my ancestral homeland of Ancient Egypt.

I had barely settled myself near the warm air conditioning duct in the Egyptology Annex of the museum when I found myself walking the sands of what might have been a beach. It was in fact, the sands and the silt between the Nile and the higher situated entrance to the Palace and the Temple complex. The silt was a result of the annual flooding of the Nile, whereas the sand came from the vast inland desert area beyond the buildings and was not subject to the flooding.

Behind me was the mighty Nile River with it's numerous papyrus-reed boats carrying single traders and the longer and more substantially built barges with their numerous oarsmen carrying their wealthy owners. And on the far shore, the ever-present papyrus reeds and the tenant farmers raising buckets full of water in order to irrigate their crops.

All around me was the noisy hustle and bustle of a marketplace. Not a market place with stalls as we would know it, but a series of streets with mud-brick houses where the occupants would barter in exchange for foods, handcrafts or household necessities.

As I walked along the street I could see fresh vegetables including grapes, onions, figs and cucumbers – and of course, wheat for grinding into flour for bread. Just ahead I could see one of the favorites outlets for the local women as well as the male servants of the Palace kitchens to visit – the honey man. I suspect that as a result of their visit, there will be some lovely edibles produced in those kitchens later today.

Another popular trading outlet was the importer of fine goods from Nubia. He knows where to obtain the finer things of life like wild animal skins, ivory, jewels and feathers and is often called to the Palace or to the home of a wealthy merchant to display his goods.

This was also the center for pilgrims from all over Egypt and beyond, to converge in order to visit the Temple to pay homage to our beloved goddess Bastet. You would know her from the beautiful statues depicting a beautiful female body with a cat's head. It was she, the daughter of the mighty and all-powerful sun god Ra, who made it possible for we cats to live in complete safety and reverence. By law none of us could be killed or injured, as that would mean death to the perpetrator – no exceptions, even if it was accidental. To humans, especially the women and the children, she was a symbol of fertility and all manner of good times and pleasures.

Pilgrims also bought their dead cats to the city for mummification and burial within the vast cemetery entirely dedicated to the eternal glory of the feline. My skin still creeps at the very thought of this entire burial ground, when re-discovered in recent modern times, being sold as phosphate, transported to other countries and used in the making of bone china. If only my mistress knew that she could be sipping her tea from the mummified remains of a

2,000-year-old Egyptian ancestor of mine!

These pilgrims also encouraged a lively trade in all things feline. As long as it had a cat image the artisans would make it and the traders would barter a sale for it. Such artifacts included decorative jars, amulets, rings, painted images on papyrus, medallions, wooden toys, bracelets and pendants, wooden combs with carved handles and statues. In fact when there was an over-supply of Temple cats the kittens were sacrificed and bartered for sale to the pilgrims as religious relics. Oh yes, trade is as old as time.

At my eye-level I could witness the bustle of this life. The peasants and farmers with their bare feet contrasted with the Palace men and women with their colorful papyrus or leather sandals. All the while I kept my eye open for my nemesis – the monkey. These were kept as pets but they did have a habit of roaming the streets and rooftops unattended. As a cat in Ancient Egypt, I was a privileged and highly beloved God. I could roam freely and safely because I knew that the human population would always respect me.

Unfortunately neither the monkey nor the baboon tribes had accepted this message. The latter were trained to climb fig trees to retrieve the fruits but they also delighted in the dropping of such fruits on any passing feline. So it was with some caution that I made my way along earthen street.

In the distance near the Temple there was a commotion. My curiosity soon had me running to the scene of the noise. The High Priest had arrived in his highly decorated chariot along with an entourage of soldiers and revered religious leaders. He was in a great hurry to get inside the Temple. I silently followed, across the canal that surrounded the building, past the grand avenue of feline statues and through the entrance between two huge and richly decorated obelisks.

What a contrast! Moving from the bright hot sunlight into the vast cool torch-lit semi-darkness. The pads of my feet could feel the coolness of the sandstone that had never felt the heat of direct sunshine. As my eyes adjusted to the dimness, I saw the High Priest moving into an anteroom. There had been a death, and lying on the block of stone in the centre of the room was the body of a beautiful pure white cat. I recognized her immediately as Sheera, the most revered and sacred cat in Bastet's Temple.

Here she lived a life akin to a goddess - divine, beautiful, svelte – and had seen the Nile flood some twenty times, a high number for any feline. The Temple initiates, the priests and the guards had already shaved their eyebrows in reverence to her passing. And now here was the High Priest on his knees, his eyes awash with tears, leading a wailing cry of loss that could be heard throughout the building. The ceremonial shaving of his eyebrows was accompanied by the haunting sounds of the reed flute and the sacred rattle, the sistrum. Every soul in the room cried at the loss of their earthly god. Sheera was on her new journey to the everlasting underworld and as such she would be lovingly prepared for that journey accompanied by everything she would require for her rebirth.

In the days that followed, her body would be mummified with exotic herbs and spices, perfumes, ointments and chemicals just the same way and with the same care and dedication as a human god would be. For her time in the tomb awaiting her rebirth, she would be sitting upright, as regal as ever. Her sarcophagus had already been prepared with the exception of some last images reflecting her final days on earth. Additional items would be prepared to accompany the body, including mummified mice for her to eat upon awakening, pots of milk, a variety of statues in her likeness, jewelry, a fine leather collar with images of Bastet engraved on it and luxurious pillows on which to recline when she was ready.

When the time was right, there would be a long three-day ceremony and celebration for her life. This was the *Ceremony of Mau,* which translates as the *Ceremony of Seeing* or the *Ceremony of the Cat.*

With the blink of an eye my sleep journey carried me forward to the finale of that event. The new God cat had ceremoniously been appointed and anointed, the all-night wailing ceremony for Sheera had been completed, as had various additional customs associated with burial and appeasement of the gods.

Along with other Temple cats, I had a prime viewing position to the side of the great gallery that housed the glorious large black bronze statue of Bastet. Her image reigned supreme from its position on the exquisitely carved marble base, her black body shining from the shaft of sunshine that pierced the dark ceiling. Her gold earrings, protective wedjat eye pendant and glistening scarab necklace, sent the viewer an immediate image of authority and god reverence.

Scattered across the entire floor were flower petals. Around the walls flaming torches – and in the corner a small band of musicians with their flutes, cymbals, hide drums and five string harps. Perfumes and incense added to the hypnotic sensual effect.

Others of the elite who waited patiently around the periphery of the gallery carried musical instruments that rattled when shaken and castanet-like devices made from bones that gave out the same urgent sound.

In front of the statue of Bastet a grand feast table had been prepared. Covered in the finest of linen cloth, it not only contained the now-mummified body of Sheera, her sarcophagus and all of the objects that would travel with her to the afterlife, there was also a banquet of food for her earth-bound mortals who would, without her living presence, celebrate the beginning of her journey. In the center of the table there burned a large green candle as a special mark of respect and reverence to Bastet.

At the appointed time through the grand entrance, the Pharaoh and High Priest led the procession of mourners into the temple. Adorned in their magnificent ceremonial robes of white and gold, of feathers and leopard skins, complete with jewelry resplendent of their God-like positions on earth, they swept forward on a tide of color. The petals swirled and danced as if the Nile breezes themselves were adding to the ceremony. The servants quickly removed the extraneous robes so that the leaders were unencumbered to do their duties. The ethereal music added to the drama and poetry of the occasion.

Prayers were called and delivered by the High Priest. The Pharaoh placed a vial of Nile water with the journey possessions.

Then like the parting of a waterway, all those on the floor separated into two groups and in through the entrance way came a young boy, the Pharaoh's eldest son. Dressed as a young warrior in white and gold, with shaved head and eyebrows and a long black hair tail, he strode with strength and preciseness to the waiting High Priest. He knelt in reverence before Bastet, and upon arising was handed a large green unlit candle. He raised the candle, lit it from the one green candle, turned to the crowd and raised it symbolically high above his head. A mighty cheer rang out from all assembled. He then walked forward and out into the burning sunshine of the Egyptian afternoon. There he lit another candle, and others came forward with more candles to be lit from the mother light.

And so the candle flame was taken and reproduced throughout the entire city so that all of the citizens could celebrate and be thankful for Sheera's earth life and for the journey she was about to begin.

Inside the temple the priests, the Pharaoh's servants, the

noblemen and the representatives of the citizens began the task of gently placing Sheera inside her gold casing that would protect her on her journey. On a stretcher of plush cushions it was placed, her head held proud and high. On other stretchers and in significant order, all her accompanying household items were readied for transport to the final ceremony at the cemetery.

To the sound of frenzied music, her bearers lifted her shoulder high and began the procession to her final resting place. Firstly it was through the temple entrance and the obelisks to say goodbye to her beloved earthly home, then along the avenue of feline statues that were festooned with garlands of flowers, across the canal bridge, through the thronging crowds and down to the water's edge and the waiting wooden barge. The highly decorated barge, along with a flotilla of one-man reed boats would travel the short distance to the cemetery and the small temple prepared for her entombment.

Inside the temple the celebrations began with food, music, dancing and joy. These are all the things Bastet enjoyed and within her bronze heart that day, she had joy in abundance.

Like my fellow felines, it didn't take me long to get from my walled perch down to the trays of milk and the freshly caught Nile fish. This was going to be a wonderful celebration when suddenly...

I became aware of a large masculine hand stroking my back and lifting me up.

"Hey, wait a minute... I haven't finished my travels," I wanted to meow. But all I heard was "Time to go home, my friend. It's closing time and I've got me rounds to do. Hurry along now. Oh, and will I see you again next week?"

My journey for today is over and I must take my leave from this warm Egyptian room - and from you. Let me share with you this beautifully written prayer to my beloved goddess Bastet that is enshrined on the wall just above where I've been sleeping. Though written by unknown hands in Ancient times it is as relevant today as then, a prayer for all who are in affinity with the peaceful feline river of life:

"Goddess Bastet, our adored and divine feline, guardian of the feminine, anointed the Serpent of Wisdom by the great god Ra – as your earth-bound guardians of the sacredness of your species, we reverently bow before you seeking blessing and benevolence.

Bring us happiness and celebration, wine and dance, music and fertility, beauty and protection.

As we walk the dark recesses of this world, bring us light.

With stealth, agility and affection protect us from the descendants of the evil serpent Apep.

And let us through your bountiful love, honor and worship the sacredness of motherhood of all living creatures."

ABOUT THE AUTHOR

Peter Benn believes in a peaceful and a loving world: a world where not only all living things co-exist in harmony and respect for one another but there is also respect for the fragile beauty and limited resources of this magnificent earth.

He writes so that we can see and appreciate the world through another's eyes.

He writes to excite imaginations, to share knowledge and to present new and loving possibilities.

Peter lives and writes in Australia. He's a mature age man who sees the world through experienced and spiritual eyes.

His affirmation is that his books will make a difference for the better.

For more about Peter and his books visit:
www.peterbenn.com

Other books by Peter Benn include paperback and e-book editions of:

EVERY DAY IS YOUR BEST DAY: Expect nothing less than wonderful!

An insightful guide to attracting happiness, abundance and spiritual joy. Combining practical life skills, a dash of religious belief, a pinch of science and perceptive New Age philosophy, this is an informative and meaningful approach to making the rest of your life, the best of your life.

"*This book was truly inspirational. I was never really into the whole 'self-help' concept, but this book really made some good points that hit-home with me.*" GoodReads Review

Mediterranean, European and Baltic CRUISE SHIP EXCURSIONS and SHORE TRIPS

Get the immediate flavor of 26 ports with this invaluable quick-look, planning guide based on the author's actual shore trip experiences. Includes an invaluable checklist of what to take with you to make your shore excursions happy and stress-free.

"*The checklist for shore excursions is particularly helpful when you're still at home and packing the things you'll need.*" Amazon Review

THE VERSATILE HUSBAND

Answers all the questions a man might ask about same-sex attraction.

"*A straightforward, practical guide for men in heterosexual relationships who'd like to explore sex with other men. Frank, honest and understanding.*" Kirkus Reviews